A Selection of Works by

**FRANZ KAFKA · DORIS LESSING
ALBERT EINSTEIN · BEATRIX POTTER
THEODOR HERZL · BOOK OF CREATION
PAUL VALERY · SAMUEL BUTLER
H. D. THOREAU · E. M. FORSTER
HANS CHRISTIAN ANDERSEN**

Selected & Edited by

LESLIE GEORGE KATZ

Fairy Tales

F O R

COMPUTERS

➤➤➤ *A Nonpareil Book* ⬅⬅⬅

Boston

ACKNOWLEDGMENTS

"The Machine Stops" from *The Eternal Moment and Other Stories* by E.M. Forster, copyright 1928 by Harcourt, Brace & World, Inc.; renewed, 1956, by E.M. Forster. Reprinted by permission of the publisher.

"The Nature Theatre of Oklahoma" from Franz Kafka, *Amerika*, translated by Edwin Muir. Copyright © 1946 by New Directions Publishing Corporation. Reprinted by permission of New Directions Publishing Corporation.

"Notes on a Dream" reprinted from *The Diaries of Theodor Herzl*, edited by Marvin Lowenthal. Copyright © 1956 by The Dial Press, Inc. and used by permission of the publisher.

The Tailor of Gloucester by Beatrix Potter, reprinted by permission of the publisher Frederick Warne & Co., Inc.

"Out of the Fountain" from *The Temptation of Jack Orkney and Other Stories* by Doris Lessing. Reprinted by permission of Curtis Brown Limited, London, on behalf of Doris Lessing.

The passages entitled "On Intelligence" by Paul Valery are from his essays "Remarks on Intelligence" and "Politics of the Mind," in *The Collected Works of Paul Valery*, edited by Jackson Mathews, Bollingen Series XLV (Princeton University Press), Volume 10, *History and Politics*, translated by Denise Folliot and Jackson Mathews (Copyright © 1962 by Bollingen Foundation). Reprinted by permission of Princeton University Press.

The aphorisms of Albert Einstein, with the exception of two, are taken from *Albert Einstein, Creator and Rebel*, by Banesh Hoffmann with the collaboration of Helen Dukas, copyright © 1972 by the authors, published by Viking Press; the sixth and seventh aphorisms in order are from "The World as I See It," originally published in *Forum and Century*, volume 84, 1930. All of the selections have been reprinted with the permission of Dr. Otto Nathan, Trustee of the Estate of Albert Einstein.

"The Nightingale" from The Heritage Press edition of *The Complete Andersen*, translated by Jean Hersholt; copyright 1942 and 1949 by The Limited Editions Club for The George Macy Companies, Inc.; used by permission.

LCC NO: 78-58450   ISBN: 0-87923-245-5

CONTENTS

FOREWORD

WHEN THE MOON was approached for the first landing by man, the computer of the lunar module began to flash alarm signals, but the astronauts found there was nothing wrong—except that the computer was having "the dithers" from being overfed information it couldn't use. Let us take pity on the poor computers of this world, often overworked and without relaxation, in the face of inordinate demands. Surely the time has come to recognize that electronic machines in a leisure-time society themselves deserve a program of recreation and entertainment, and even edification. Computers too have their problems, and are vulnerable. Some of the latest models come with a human being attached for nine months to help the machine adjust to existence. The relation of man and computer is interdependence. They should strive to understand one another better. Here then is what may be the first book of fairy tales, philosophical thoughts and classic comments on the subject, published for computers in a computerized world.

In electronic terms the stories, essays and romances are pre-historic. Yet every race needs a mythos of tradition: Perhaps this collection may be viewed as semi-sacred prophetic writings that will help give computers a sense of religious origin and historic identity.

Sometimes men appear in these fictions and essays as threatened or struggling beings, embattled gods defending themselves against mortal machineries they have created. If computers have the status of minor deities, it should at least be remembered that gods and mortals have always been rivals, and the universe has best thrived —at least in fairy tales—when the competition is friendly.

The selections chosen have all inevitably and by necessity been written by men rather than by machines. The time has not quite arrived when machines write their own fantasies for the delectation and instruction of humans, for consumers to applaud and give themselves over to, and for the benefit of commerce—though manufacturers of computers we may be sure are working hard on that potentially lucrative development. Mankind's stubborn tendency to remain anthropomorphic is difficult to absolutely eradicate, despite the reactionary curb an obsession with non-commercial values places on research and marketing. Machines reading this work will, it is hoped, make allowances for the primeval ire of those authors who treat the lives of individual humans as somehow more precious or vital than machines, and who write as if the ascendancy of machinery over humans is something to be fought instead of accepted.

Admittedly most of these authors are pre-electronic, and therefore antemundane. E. M. Forster wrote "The Machine Stops" before the First World War began. Kafka invented his bureaucratic wonderland for worker-entertainers in the same epoch; his never-never land serves to indicate that humans must face questions of vocation, recreation and community that computers have hardly any idea of. Computers inhabit a virtual utopia, whereas people such as the confrères of Theodor Herzl have the same difficulties Herzl was trying to solve in eighteen ninety-five when he jotted notes for what he believed might be either a romantic fantasy or a practical plan for a modern humanist machine state. Again before the twentieth century arrived, Samuel Butler wrote (by hand) "The Book of the Machine," which dared infidelism by imagining a country called Erewhon where the inhabitants enjoyed an advanced happiness because all machines including calculating devices had been destroyed and banished by law. Any nation today might conceivably banish certain kinds of innocent humans, but outlaw innocent machines? Never.

Even earlier, in eighteen fifty-one, Henry David

Thoreau was revolting against the Industrial Revolution well before the American Civil War, a struggle about individual freedom which did much to advance the cause of engineering. Thoreau's blasphemy was to oppose the projection of a computer state as paradise and to insist that the mechanics of nature offered incalculable rewards infinitely superior to the wildest dreams of the computable.

Some fairy tales, although written exclusively for humans, pay high compliments to measurable quantities, and recognize the finite as a determining factor of human well-being. In *The Tailor of Gloucester* the amount of cherry-coloured twist available to complete the buttonholes of a fancy vest sewn by compassionate mice is of crucial importance. The relevance of Doris Lessing's story "Out of the Fountain," the most recently written parable in this book, deserves attention. Viz: A computer may someday soon learn to split a diamond, but will it ever as the diamond cutter in the story does learn to value the beauty and perfection of a pearl? The pearl's worth is beyond computation; its perfection exists apart from personal fate. The hero believes that when the heroine direly needed money, she should have sold the pearl instead of turning it into an object of sentiment. (Computers may be described as being sentimental about integers and sums.)

Paul Valéry's uncomplimentary remarks, written in the nineteen thirties, are apocalyptic. His attack on machines and his defense of humane intelligence is a proclamation of crisis. Valéry is a virulent and dangerous thinker whose subversive ideas computers had better keep a watch on. His writings are a threat to every button available to be pushed.

Albert Einstein is probably the foremost human computer produced in the twentieth century, and he agrees with Thoreau: he proclaims the ascendancy of ethics over physics. (Can we teach the computer to love?) Einstein tells us he arrived at his theory of relativity *by intuition*.

The origin of the universe as created by God in the Old Testament deserves to be included. God flattered statistics by making the firmament, the earth, and living things including humanity in six days, and then had the grace to add a seventh so that man could rest from counting.

Perhaps the ultimate fairy tale for computers is "The Nightingale" by Hans Christian Andersen. It outlines the basic distinction between the race of electronic beings and the human race, distinguishing the fatal qualities inherent in creatures of flesh and blood. While our life spans are of limited duration (as are those of computers), we are never capable of being completely programmed (as computers always are). Living beings live in uncertainty, are doomed to the delights of confusion, and the despairs of enduring the unexpected.

To define the subject and the issue in desperate terms, we live in an age of esthetic fascism, when human exploiters have learned to give a statistical excuse for every perfidy, when philistines equate the arbitrary with the brutal as a matter of course, resting their mystic claims on statistic necessity. In the cause of truth computers are innocent bystanders. The war of values is a civil war between human beings. If only we could teach computation itself the value of conscience, which is the essence of amusement! As for moral meaning, it is ever present: it is the human element.

While this book is published primarily for computers and their machine in-laws in a world they already dominate, persons whose duty it is to serve computers and to tend machines, even those persons who are believed to be fully affiliated or completely enmeshed, may take pleasure in reading it for their own private purposes. At least, respectfully, this possibility, instead of being ruled out, is counted on by

THE EDITOR.

THE MACHINE STOPS

E. M. Forster

I. THE AIR-SHIP

IMAGINE, if you can, a small room, hexagonal in shape, like the cell of a bee. It is lighted neither by window nor by lamp, yet it is filled with a soft radiance. There are no apertures for ventilation, yet the air is fresh. There are no musical instruments, and yet, at the moment that my meditation opens, this room is throbbing with melodious sounds. An arm-chair is in the centre, by its side a reading-desk —that is all the furniture. And in the arm-chair there sits a swaddled lump of flesh—a woman, about five feet high, with a face as white as a fungus. It is to her that the little room belongs.

An electric bell rang.

The woman touched a switch and the music was silent.

"I suppose I must see who it is," she thought, and set her chair in motion. The chair, like the music, was worked by machinery, and it rolled her to the other side of the room, where the bell still rang importunately.

"Who is it?" she called. Her voice was irritable, for she had been interrupted often since the music began. She knew several thousand people; in certain directions human intercourse had advanced enormously.

But when she listened into the receiver, her white face wrinkled into smiles, and she said:

"Very well. Let us talk, I will isolate myself. I do not expect anything important will happen for the next five minutes—for I can give you fully five minutes, Kuno. Then I must deliver my lecture on 'Music during the Australian Period.' "

She touched the isolation knob, so that no one else could speak to her. Then she touched the lighting apparatus, and the little room was plunged into darkness.

"Be quick!" she called, her irritation returning. "Be quick, Kuno; here I am in the dark wasting my time."

But it was fully fifteen seconds before the round plate that she held in her hands began to glow. A faint blue light shot across it, darkening to purple, and presently she could see the image of her son, who lived on the other side of the earth, and he could see her.

"Kuno, how slow you are."

He smiled gravely.

"I really believe you enjoy dawdling."

"I have called you before, mother, but you were always busy or isolated. I have something particular to say."

"What is it, dearest boy? Be quick. Why could you not send it by pneumatic post?"

"Because I prefer saying such a thing. I want——"

"Well?"

"I want you to come and see me."

Vashti watched his face in the blue plate.

"But I can see you!" she exclaimed. "What more do you want?"

"I want to see you not through the Machine," said Kuno. "I want to speak to you not through the wearisome Machine."

"Oh, hush!" said his mother, vaguely shocked.

"You mustn't say anything against the Machine."

"Why not?"

"One mustn't."

"You talk as if a god had made the Machine," cried the other. "I believe that you pray to it when you are unhappy. Men made it, do not forget that. Great men, but men. The Machine is much, but it is not everything. I see something like you in this plate, but I do not see you. I hear something like you through this telephone, but I do not hear you. That is why I want you to come. Come and stop with me. Pay me a visit, so that we can meet face to face, and talk about the hopes that are in my mind."

She replied that she could scarcely spare the time for a visit.

"The air-ship barely takes two days to fly between me and you."

"I dislike air-ships."

"Why?"

"I dislike seeing the horrible brown earth, and the sea, and the stars when it is dark. I get no ideas in an air-ship."

"I do not get them anywhere else."

"What kind of ideas can the air give you?"

He paused for an instant.

"Do you not know four big stars that form an oblong, and three stars close together in the middle of the oblong, and hanging from these stars, three other stars?"

"No, I do not. I dislike the stars. But did they give you an idea? How interesting; tell me."

"I had an idea that they were like a man."

"I do not understand."

"The four big stars are the man's shoulders and his knees. The three stars in the middle are like the belts that men wore once, and the three stars hanging are like a sword."

"A sword?"

"Men carried swords about with them, to kill animals and other men."

"It does not strike me as a very good idea, but it is certainly original. When did it come to you first?"

"In the air-ship——" He broke off, and she fancied that he looked sad. She could not be sure, for the Machine did not transmit *nuances* of expression. It only gave a general idea of people—an idea that was good enough for all practical purposes, Vashti thought. The imponderable bloom, declared by a discredited philosophy to be the actual essence of intercourse, was rightly ignored by the Machine, just as the imponderable bloom of the grape was ignored by the manufacturers of artificial fruit. Something "good enough" had long since been accepted by our race.

"The truth is," he continued, "that I want to see these stars again. They are curious stars. I want to see them not from the air-ship, but from the surface of the earth, as our ancestors did, thousands of years ago. I want to visit the surface of the earth."

She was shocked again.

"Mother, you must come, if only to explain to me what is the harm of visiting the surface of the earth."

"No harm," she replied, controlling herself. "But no advantage. The surface of the earth is only dust and mud, no life remains on it, and you would need a respirator, or the cold of the outer air would kill you. One dies immediately in the outer air."

"I know; of course I shall take all precautions."

"And besides——"

"Well?"

She considered, and chose her words with care.

Her son had a queer temper, and she wished to dissuade him from the expedition.

"It is contrary to the spirit of the age," she asserted.

"Do you mean by that, contrary to the Machine?"

"In a sense, but——"

His image in the blue plate faded.

"Kuno!"

He had isolated himself.

For a moment Vashti felt lonely.

Then she generated the light, and the sight of her room, flooded with radiance and studded with electric buttons, revived her. There were buttons and switches everywhere—buttons to call for food, for music, for clothing. There was the hot-bath button, by pressure of which a basin of (imitation) marble rose out of the floor, filled to the brim with a warm deodorised liquid. There was the cold-bath button. There was the button that produced literature. And there were of course the buttons by which she communicated with her friends. The room, though it contained nothing, was in touch with all that she cared for in the world.

Vashti's next move was to turn off the isolation-switch, and all the accumulations of the last three minutes burst upon her. The room was filled with the noise of bells, and speaking-tubes. What was the new food like? Could she recommend it? Had she had any ideas lately? Might one tell her one's own ideas? Would she make an engagement to visit the public nurseries at an early date?—say this day month.

To most of these questions she replied with irritation—a growing quality in that accelerated age. She said that the new food was horrible. That she could not visit the public nurseries through press of engagements. That she had no ideas of her own but had just been told one—that four stars and three in the middle were like a man: she doubted there was much in it. Then she switched off her correspondents, for it was time to deliver her lecture on Australian music.

The clumsy system of public gatherings had been long since abandoned; neither Vashti nor her audience stirred from their rooms. Seated in her armchair she spoke, while they in their arm-chairs heard her, fairly well, and saw her, fairly well. She opened with a humorous account of music in the pre-Mongolian epoch, and went on to describe the great outburst of song that followed the Chinese conquest. Remote and primæval as were the methods of I-San-So and the Brisbane school, she yet felt (she said) that study of them might repay the musician of today: they had freshness; they had, above all, ideas.

Her lecture, which lasted ten minutes, was well received, and at its conclusion she and many of her audience listened to a lecture on the sea; there were ideas to be got from the sea; the speaker had donned a respirator and visited it lately. Then she fed, talked to many friends, had a bath, talked again, and summoned her bed.

The bed was not to her liking. It was too large, and she had a feeling for a small bed. Complaint was useless, for beds were of the same dimension all over the world, and to have had an alternative size would have involved vast alterations in the Machine. Vashti isolated herself—it was necessary, for neither day nor night existed under the ground—and reviewed all that had happened since she had summoned the bed last. Ideas? Scarcely any. Events—was Kuno's invitation an event?

By her side, on the little reading-desk, was a survival from the ages of litter—one book. This was the Book of the Machine. In it were instructions against every possible contingency. If she was hot or cold or dyspeptic or at loss for a word, she went to the book, and it told her which button to press. The Central Committee published it. In accordance with a growing habit, it was richly bound.

Sitting up in the bed, she took it reverently in her hands. She glanced round the glowing room as if some one might be watching her. Then, half ashamed, half joyful, she murmured "O Machine! O Machine!" and raised the volume to her lips. Thrice she kissed it, thrice inclined her head, thrice she felt the delirium of acquiescence. Her ritual performed, she turned to page 1367, which gave the times of the departure of the air-ships from the island in the southern hemisphere, under whose soil she lived, to the island in the northern hemisphere, whereunder lived her son.

She thought, "I have not the time."

She made the room dark and slept; she awoke and made the room light; she ate and exchanged ideas with her friends, and listened to music and attended lectures; she made the room dark and slept. Above her, beneath her, and around her, the Machine hummed eternally; she did not notice the noise, for she had been born with it in her ears. The earth, carrying her, hummed as it sped through silence, turning her now to the invisible sun, now to the invisible stars. She awoke and made the room light.

"Kuno!"

"I will not talk to you," he answered, "until you come."

"Have you been on the surface of the earth since we spoke last?"

His image faded.

Again she consulted the book. She became very nervous and lay back in her chair palpitating. Think of her as without teeth or hair. Presently she directed the chair to the wall, and pressed an unfamiliar button. The wall swung apart slowly. Through the opening she saw a tunnel that curved slightly, so that its goal was not visible. Should she go to see her son, here was the beginning of the journey.

Of course she knew all about the communication-system. There was nothing mysterious in it. She would summon a car and it would fly with her down the tunnel until it reached the lift that communicated with the air-ship station: the system had been in use for many, many years, long before the universal establishment of the Machine. And of course she had studied the civilisation that had immediately preceded her own—the civilisation that had mistaken the functions of the system, and had used it for bringing people to things, instead of for bringing things to people. Those funny old days, when men went for change of air instead of changing the air in their rooms! And yet—she was frightened of the tunnel: she had not seen it since her last child was born. It curved—but not quite as she remembered; it was brilliant—but not quite as brilliant as a lecturer had suggested. Vashti was seized with the terrors of direct experience. She shrank back into the room, and the wall closed up again.

"Kuno," she said, "I cannot come to see you. I am not well."

Immediately an enormous apparatus fell on to her out of the ceiling, a thermometer was automatically inserted between her lips, a stethoscope was automatically laid upon her heart. She lay powerless. Cool pads soothed her forehead. Kuno had telegraphed to her doctor.

So the human passions still blundered up and down in the Machine. Vashti drank the medicine that the doctor projected into her mouth, and the machinery retired into the ceiling. The voice of Kuno was heard asking how she felt.

"Better." Then with irritation: "But why do you not come to me instead?"

"Because I cannot leave this place."

"Why?"

"Because, any moment, something tremendous may happen."

"Have you been on the surface of the earth yet?"

"Not yet."

"Then what is it?"

"I will not tell you through the Machine."

She resumed her life.

But she thought of Kuno as a baby, his birth, his removal to the public nurseries, her one visit to him there, his visits to her—visits which stopped when the Machine had assigned him a room on the other side of the earth. "Parents, duties of," said the book of the Machine, "cease at the moment of birth. P. 422327483." True, but there was something special about Kuno—indeed there had been something special about all her children—and, after all, she must brave the journey if he desired it. And "something tremendous might happen." What did that mean? The nonsense of a youthful man, no doubt, but she must go. Again she pressed the unfamiliar button, again the wall swung back, and she saw the tunnel that curved out of sight. Clasping the Book, she rose, tottered on to the platform, and summoned the car. Her room closed behind her: the journey to the northern hemisphere had begun.

Of course it was perfectly easy. The car approached and in it she found arm-chairs exactly like her own. When she signalled, it stopped, and she tottered into the lift. One other passenger was in the lift, the first fellow creature she had seen face to face for months. Few travelled in these days, for, thanks to the advance of science, the earth was exactly alike all over. Rapid intercourse, from which the previous civilisation had hoped so much, had ended by defeating itself. What was the good of going to Pekin when it was just like Shrewsbury? Why return to Shrewsbury when it would be just like Pekin? Men seldom moved their bodies; all unrest was concentrated in the soul.

The air-ship service was a relic from the former age. It was kept up, because it was easier to keep it up than to stop it or to diminish it, but it now far exceeded the wants of the population. Vessel after vessel would rise from the vomitories of Rye or of Christchurch (I use the antique names), would sail into the crowded sky, and would draw up at the wharves of the south—empty. So nicely adjusted was the system, so independent of meteorology, that the sky, whether calm or cloudy, resembled a vast kaleidoscope whereon the same patterns periodically recurred. The ship on which Vashti sailed started now at sunset, now at dawn. But always, as it passed above Rheims, it would neighbour the ship that served between Helsingfors and the Brazils, and, every third time it surmounted the Alps, the fleet of Palermo would cross its track behind. Night and day, wind and storm, tide and earthquake, impeded man no longer. He had harnessed Leviathan. All the old literature, with its praise of Nature, and its fear of Nature, rang false as the prattle of a child.

Yet as Vashti saw the vast flank of the ship, stained with exposure to the outer air, her horror of direct experience returned. It was not quite like the air-ship in the cinematophote. For one thing it smelt—not strongly or unpleasantly, but it did smell, and with her eyes shut she should have known that a new thing was close to her. Then she had to walk to it from the lift, had to submit to glances from the other passengers. The man in front dropped his Book—no great matter, but it disquieted them all. In the rooms, if the Book was dropped, the floor raised it mechanically, but the gangway to the air-ship was not so prepared, and the sacred volume lay motionless. They stopped—the thing was unforeseen—and the man, instead of picking up his property, felt the muscles of his arm to see how they had failed him. Then some one actually said with direct utterance: "We shall be late"—and they trooped on board, Vashti treading on the pages as she did so.

Inside, her anxiety increased. The arrangements were old-fashioned and rough. There was even a female attendant, to whom she would have to announce her wants during the voyage. Of course a revolving platform ran the length of the boat, but she was expected to walk from it to her cabin. Some cabins were better than others, and she did not get the best. She thought the attendant had been unfair, and spasms of rage shook her. The glass valves had closed, she could not go back. She saw, at the end of the vestibule, the lift in which she had ascended going quietly up and down, empty. Beneath those corridors of shining tiles were rooms, tier below tier, reaching far into the earth, and in each room there sat a human being, eating, or sleeping, or producing ideas. And buried deep in the hive was her own room. Vashti was afraid.

"O Machine! O Machine!" she murmured, and caressed her Book, and was comforted.

Then the sides of the vestibule seemed to melt together, as do the passages that we see in dreams, the lift vanished, the Book that had been dropped slid to the left and vanished, polished tiles rushed by like a stream of water, there was a slight jar, and the airship, issuing from its tunnel, soared above the waters of a tropical ocean.

It was night. For a moment she saw the coast of Sumatra edged by the phosphorescence of waves, and crowned by lighthouses, still sending forth their disregarded beams. These also vanished, and only the stars distracted her. They were not motionless, but swayed to and fro above her head, thronging out of one skylight into another, as if the universe and not the air-ship was careening. And, as often happens on clear nights, they seemed now to be in perspective, now on a plane; now piled tier beyond tier into the infinite heavens, now concealing infinity, a roof limiting for ever the visions of men. In either case they seemed intolerable. "Are we to travel in the dark?" called the passengers angrily, and the attendant, who had been careless, generated the light, and pulled down the blinds of pliable metal. When the air-ships had been built, the desire to look direct at things still lingered in the world. Hence the extraordinary number of skylights and windows, and the proportionate discomfort to those who were civilised and refined. Even in Vashti's cabin one star peeped through a flaw in the blind, and after a few hours' uneasy slumber, she was disturbed by an unfamiliar glow, which was the dawn.

Quick as the ship had sped westwards, the earth had rolled eastwards quicker still, and had dragged back Vashti and her companions towards the sun. Science could prolong the night, but only for a little, and those high hopes of neutralising the earth's diurnal revolution had passed, together with hopes that were possibly higher. To "keep pace with the sun," or even to outstrip it, had been the aim of the civilisation preceding this. Racing aeroplanes had been built for the purpose, capable of enormous speed, and steered by the greatest intellects of the epoch. Round the globe they went, round and round, westward, westward, round and round, amidst humanity's applause. In vain. The globe went eastward quicker still, horrible accidents occurred, and the Committee of the Machine, at the time rising into prominence, declared the pursuit illegal, unmechanical, and punishable by Homelessness.

Of Homelessness more will be said later.

Doubtless the Committee was right. Yet the attempt to "defeat the sun" aroused the last common interest that our race experienced about the heavenly bodies, or indeed about anything. It was the last time that men were compacted by thinking of a power outside the world. The sun had conquered, yet it was the end of his spiritual dominion. Dawn, midday, twilight, the zodiacal path, touched neither men's lives nor their hearts, and science retreated into the ground, to concentrate herself upon problems that she was certain of solving.

So when Vashti found her cabin invaded by a rosy finger of light, she was annoyed, and tried to adjust the blind. But the blind flew up altogether, and she saw through the skylight small pink clouds, swaying against a background of blue, and as the sun crept higher, its radiance entered direct, brimming down the wall, like a golden sea. It rose and fell with the air-ship's motion, just as waves rise and fall, but it advanced steadily, as a tide advances. Unless she was careful, it would strike her face. A spasm of horror shook her and she rang for the attendant. The attendant too was horrified, but she could do nothing; it was not her place to mend the blind. She could only suggest that the lady should change her cabin, which she accordingly prepared to do.

People were almost exactly alike all over the world, but the attendant of the air-ship, perhaps owing to her exceptional duties, had grown a little out of the common. She had often to address passengers with direct speech, and this had given her a certain roughness and originality of manner. When Vashti swerved away from the sunbeams with a cry, she behaved barbarically—she put out her hand to steady her.

"How dare you!" exclaimed the passenger. "You forget yourself!"

The woman was confused, and apologised for not having let her fall. People never touched one another. The custom had become obsolete, owing to the Machine.

"Where are we now?" asked Vashti haughtily.

"We are over Asia," said the attendant, anxious to be polite.

"Asia?"

"You must excuse my common way of speaking. I have got into the habit of calling places over which I pass by their unmechanical names."

"Oh, I remember Asia. The Mongols came from it."

"Beneath us, in the open air, stood a city that was once called Simla."

"Have you ever heard of the Mongols and of the Brisbane school?"

"No."

"Brisbane also stood in the open air."

"Those mountains to the right—let me show you them." She pushed back a metal blind. The main chain of the Himalayas was revealed. "They were once called the Roof of the World, those mountains."

"What a foolish name!"

"You must remember that, before the dawn of civilisation, they seemed to be an impenetrable wall that touched the stars. It was supposed that no one but the gods could exist above their summits. How we have advanced, thanks to the Machine!"

"How we have advanced, thanks to the Machine!" said Vashti.

"How we have advanced, thanks to the Machine!" echoed the passenger who had dropped his Book the night before, and who was standing in the passage.

"And that white stuff in the cracks?—what is it?"

"I have forgotten its name."

"Cover the window, please. These mountains give me no ideas."

The northern aspect of the Himalayas was in deep shadow: on the Indian slope the sun had just prevailed. The forests had been destroyed during the literature epoch for the purpose of making newspaper-pulp, but the snows were awakening to their morning glory, and clouds still hung on the breasts of Kinchinjunga. In the plain were seen the ruins of cities, with diminished rivers creeping by their walls, and by the sides of these were sometimes the signs of vomitories, marking the cities of today. Over the whole prospect air-ships rushed, crossing and inter-crossing with incredible *aplomb*, and rising noncha-lantly when they desired to escape the perturbations of the lower atmosphere and to traverse the Roof of the World.

"We have indeed advanced, thanks to the Ma-chine," repeated the attendant, and hid the Himala-yas behind a metal blind.

The day dragged wearily forward. The passengers sat each in his cabin, avoiding one another with an almost physical repulsion and longing to be once more under the surface of the earth. There were eight or ten of them, mostly young males, sent out from the public nurseries to inhabit the rooms of those who had died in various parts of the earth. The man who had dropped his Book was on the home-ward journey. He had been sent to Sumatra for the purpose of propagating the race. Vashti alone was travelling by her private will.

At midday she took a second glance at the earth.

The air-ship was crossing another range of mountains, but she could see little, owing to clouds. Masses of black rock hovered below her, and merged indistinctly into grey. Their shapes were fantastic; one of them resembled a prostrate man.

"No ideas here," murmured Vashti, and hid the Caucasus behind a metal blind.

In the evening she looked again. They were crossing a golden sea, in which lay many small islands and one peninsula.

She repeated, "No ideas here," and hid Greece behind a metal blind.

II. THE MENDING APPARATUS

By a vestibule, by a lift, by a tubular railway, by a platform, by a sliding door—by reversing all the steps of her departure did Vashti arrive at her son's room, which exactly resembled her own. She might well declare that the visit was superfluous. The buttons, the knobs, the reading-desk with the Book, the temperature, the atmosphere, the illumination—all were exactly the same. And if Kuno himself, flesh of her flesh, stood close beside her at last, what profit was there in that? She was too well-bred to shake him by the hand.

Averting her eyes, she spoke as follows:

"Here I am. I have had the most terrible journey and greatly retarded the development of my soul. It is not worth it, Kuno, it is not worth it. My time is too precious. The sunlight almost touched me, and I have met with the rudest people. I can only stop a few minutes. Say what you want to say, and then I must return."

"I have been threatened with Homelessness," said Kuno.

She looked at him now.

"I have been threatened with Homelessness, and I could not tell you such a thing through the Machine."

Homelessness means death. The victim is exposed to the air, which kills him.

"I have been outside since I spoke to you last. The tremendous thing has happened, and they have discovered me."

"But why shouldn't you go outside!" she exclaimed. "It is perfectly legal, perfectly mechanical, to visit the surface of the earth. I have lately been to a lecture on the sea; there is no objection to that; one simply summons a respirator and gets an Egression-permit. It is not the kind of thing that spiritually-minded people do, and I begged you not to do it, but there is no legal objection to it."

"I did not get an Egression-permit."

"Then how did you get out?"

"I found out a way of my own."

The phrase conveyed no meaning to her, and he had to repeat it.

"A way of your own?" she whispered. "But that would be wrong."

"Why?"

The question shocked her beyond measure.

"You are beginning to worship the Machine," he said coldly. "You think it irreligious of me to have found out a way of my own. It was just what the Committee thought, when they threatened me with Homelessness."

At this she grew angry. "I worship nothing!" she cried. "I am most advanced. I don't think you irre-ligious, for there is no such thing as religion left. All the fear and the superstition that existed once have been destroyed by the Machine. I only meant that to find out a way of your own was—— Besides, there is no new way out."

"So it is always supposed."

"Except through the vomitories, for which one must have an Egression-permit, it is impossible to get out. The Book says so."

"Well, the Book's wrong, for I have been out on my feet."

For Kuno was possessed of a certain physical strength.

By these days it was a demerit to be muscular. Each infant was examined at birth, and all who promised undue strength were destroyed. Humanitarians may protest, but it would have been no true kindness to let an athlete live; he would never have been happy in that state of life to which the Machine had called him; he would have yearned for trees to climb, rivers to bathe in, meadows and hills against which he might measure his body. Man must be adapted to his surroundings, must he not? In the dawn of the world our weakly must be exposed on Mount Taygetus, in its twilight our strong will suffer euthanasia, that the Machine may progress, that the Machine may progress, that the Machine may progress eternally.

"You know that we have lost the sense of space. We say 'space is annihilated,' but we have annihilated not space, but the sense thereof. We have lost a part of ourselves. I determined to recover it, and I began by walking up and down the platform of the railway outside my room. Up and down, until I was tired, and so did recapture the meaning of 'Near' and 'Far.' 'Near' is a place to which I can get quickly *on my feet*, not a place to which the train or the airship will take me quickly. 'Far' is a place to which I cannot get quickly on my feet; the vomitory is 'far,' though I could be there in thirty-eight seconds by summoning the train. Man is the measure. That was my first lesson. Man's feet are the measure for distance, his hands are the measure for ownership, his body is the measure for all that is lovable and desirable and strong. Then I went further: it was then that I called to you for the first time, and you would not come.

"This city, as you know, is built deep beneath the surface of the earth, with only the vomitories protruding. Having paced the platform outside my own room, I took the lift to the next platform and paced that also, and so with each in turn, until I came to the topmost, above which begins the earth. All the platforms were exactly alike, and all that I gained by visiting them was to develop my sense of space and my muscles. I think I should have been content with this—it is not a little thing—but as I walked and brooded, it occurred to me that our cities had been built in the days when men still breathed the outer air, and that there had been ventilation shafts for the workmen. I could think of nothing but these ventilation shafts. Had they been destroyed by all the food-tubes and medicine-tubes and music-tubes that the Machine has evolved lately? Or did traces of them remain? One thing was certain. If I came upon them anywhere, it would be in the railway-tunnels of the topmost story. Everywhere else, all space was accounted for.

"I am telling my story quickly, but don't think that I was not a coward or that your answers never depressed me. It is not the proper thing, it is not mechanical, it is not decent to walk along a railway-tunnel. I did not fear that I might tread upon a live rail and be killed. I feared something far more in-

29

tangible—doing what was not contemplated by the Machine. Then I said to myself, 'Man is the measure,' and I went, and after many visits I found an opening.

"The tunnels, of course, were lighted. Everything is light, artificial light; darkness is the exception. So when I saw a black gap in the tiles, I knew that it was an exception, and rejoiced. I put in my arm—I could put in no more at first—and waved it round and round in ecstasy. I loosened another tile, and put in my head, and shouted into the darkness: 'I am coming, I shall do it yet,' and my voice reverberated down endless passages. I seemed to hear the spirits of those dead workmen who had returned each evening to the starlight and to their wives, and all the generations who had lived in the open air called back to me, 'You will do it yet, you are coming.' "

He paused, and, absurd as he was, his last words moved her. For Kuno had lately asked to be a father, and his request had been refused by the Committee. His was not a type that the Machine desired to hand on.

"Then a train passed. It brushed by me, but I thrust my head and arms into the hole. I had done enough for one day, so I crawled back to the platform, went down in the lift, and summoned my bed. Ah, what dreams! And again I called you, and again you refused."

She shook her head and said:

"Don't. Don't talk of these terrible things. You make me miserable. You are throwing civilisation away."

"But I had got back the sense of space and a man cannot rest then. I determined to get in at the hole and climb the shaft. And so I exercised my arms. Day after day I went through ridiculous movements, until my flesh ached, and I could hang by my hands and hold the pillow of my bed outstretched for many minutes. Then I summoned a respirator, and started.

"It was easy at first. The mortar had somehow rotted, and I soon pushed some more tiles in, and clambered after them into the darkness, and the spirits of the dead comforted me. I don't know what I mean by that. I just say what I felt. I felt, for the first time, that a protest had been lodged against corruption, and that even as the dead were comforting me, so I was comforting the unborn. I felt that humanity existed, and that it existed without clothes. How can I possibly explain this? It was naked, humanity seemed naked, and all these tubes and buttons and machineries neither came into the world with us, nor will they follow us out, nor do they matter supremely while we are here. Had I been strong, I would have torn off every garment I had, and gone out into the outer air unswaddled. But this is not for me, nor perhaps for my generation. I climbed with my respirator and my hygienic clothes and my dietetic tabloids! Better thus than not at all.

"There was a ladder, made of some primæval metal. The light from the railway fell upon its lowest rungs, and I saw that it led straight upwards out of the rubble at the bottom of the shaft. Perhaps our ancestors ran up and down it a dozen times daily, in their building. As I climbed, the rough edges cut through my gloves so that my hands bled. The light helped me for a little, and then came darkness and, worse still, silence which pierced my ears like a sword. The Machine hums! Did you know that? Its hum penetrates our blood, and may even guide our thoughts. Who knows! I was getting beyond its power. Then I thought: 'This silence means that I am doing wrong.' But I heard voices in the silence, and again they strengthened me." He laughed. "I had need of them. The next moment I cracked my head against something."

She sighed.

"I had reached one of those pneumatic stoppers that defend us from the outer air. You may have noticed them on the air-ship. Pitch dark, my feet on the rungs of an invisible ladder, my hands cut; I cannot explain how I lived through this part, but the voices still comforted me, and I felt for fastenings. The stopper, I suppose, was about eight feet across. I passed my hand over it as far as I could reach. It was perfectly smooth. I felt it almost to the centre. Not quite to the centre, for my arm was too short. Then the voice said: 'Jump. It is worth it. There may be a handle in the centre, and you may catch hold of it and so come to us your own way. And if there is no handle, so that you may fall and are dashed to pieces —it is still worth it: you will still come to us your own way.' So I jumped. There was a handle, and ———"

He paused. Tears gathered in his mother's eyes. She knew that he was fated. If he did not die today he would die tomorrow. There was not room for such a person in the world. And with her pity disgust mingled. She was ashamed at having borne such a son, she who had always been so respectable and so full of ideas. Was he really the little boy to whom she had taught the use of his stops and buttons, and to whom she had given his first lessons in the Book? The very hair that disfigured his lip showed that he was reverting to some savage type. On atavism the Machine can have no mercy.

"There was a handle, and I did catch it. I hung tranced over the darkness and heard the hum of these workings as the last whisper in a dying dream. All the things I had cared about and all the people I had spoken to through tubes appeared infinitely little. Meanwhile the handle revolved. My weight had set something in motion and I span slowly, and then——

"I cannot describe it. I was lying with my face to the sunshine. Blood poured from my nose and ears and I heard a tremendous roaring. The stopper, with me clinging to it, had simply been blown out of the earth, and the air that we make down here was escaping through the vent into the air above. It burst up like a fountain. I crawled back to it—for the upper air hurts—and, as it were, I took great sips from the edge. My respirator had flown goodness knows where, my clothes were torn. I just lay with my lips close to the hole, and I sipped until the bleeding stopped. You can imagine nothing so curious. This hollow in the grass—I will speak of it in a minute,—the sun shining into it, not brilliantly but through marbled clouds,—the peace, the nonchalance, the sense of space, and, brushing my cheek, the roaring fountain of our artificial air! Soon I spied my respirator, bobbing up and down in the current high above my head, and higher still were many airships. But no one ever looks out of air-ships, and in my case they could not have picked me up. There I was, stranded. The sun shone a little way down the shaft, and revealed the topmost rung of the ladder, but it was hopeless trying to reach it. I should either have been tossed up again by the escape, or else have fallen in, and died. I could only lie on the grass, sipping and sipping, and from time to time glancing around me.

"I knew that I was in Wessex, for I had taken care to go to a lecture on the subject before starting.

Wessex lies above the room in which we are talking now. It was once an important state. Its kings held all the southern coast from the Andredswald to Cornwall, while the Wansdyke protected them on the north, running over the high ground. The lecturer was only concerned with the rise of Wessex, so I do not know how long it remained an international power, nor would the knowledge have assisted me. To tell the truth I could do nothing but laugh, during this part. There was I, with a pneumatic stopper by my side and a respirator bobbing over my head, imprisoned, all three of us, in a grass-grown hollow that was edged with fern."

Then he grew grave again.

"Lucky for me that it was a hollow. For the air began to fall back into it and to fill it as water fills a bowl. I could crawl about. Presently I stood. I breathed a mixture, in which the air that hurts predominated whenever I tried to climb the sides. This was not so bad. I had not lost my tabloids and remained ridiculously cheerful, and as for the Machine, I forgot about it altogether. My one aim now was to get to the top, where the ferns were, and to view whatever objects lay beyond.

"I rushed the slope. The new air was still too bitter for me and I came rolling back, after a momentary vision of something grey. The sun grew very feeble, and I remembered that he was in Scorpio—I had been to a lecture on that too. If the sun is in Scorpio and you are in Wessex, it means that you must be as quick as you can, or it will get too dark. (This is the first bit of useful information I have ever got from a lecture, and I expect it will be the last.) It made me try frantically to breathe the new air, and to advance as far as I dared out of my pond. The hollow filled so slowly. At times I thought that the fountain played with less vigour. My respirator seemed to dance nearer the earth; the roar was decreasing."

He broke off.

"I don't think this is interesting you. The rest will interest you even less. There are no ideas in it, and I wish that I had not troubled you to come. We are too different, mother."

She told him to continue.

"It was evening before I climbed the bank. The sun had very nearly slipped out of the sky by this time, and I could not get a good view. You, who have just crossed the Roof of the World, will not want to hear an account of the little hills that I saw—low colourless hills. But to me they were living and the turf that covered them was a skin, under which their muscles rippled, and I felt that those hills had called with incalculable force to men in the past, and that men had loved them. Now they sleep—perhaps for ever. They commune with humanity in dreams. Happy the man, happy the woman, who awakes the hills of Wessex. For though they sleep, they will never die."

His voice rose passionately.

"Cannot you see, cannot all your lecturers see, that it is we who are dying, and that down here the only thing that really lives is the Machine? We created the Machine, to do our will, but we cannot make it do our will now. It has robbed us of the sense of space and of the sense of touch, it has blurred every human relation and narrowed down love to a carnal act, it has paralysed our bodies and our wills, and now it compels us to worship it. The Machine develops—but not on our lines. The Machine proceeds—but not to our goal. We only exist as the blood corpuscles that course through its arteries, and if it could work without us, it would let us die. Oh,

I have no remedy—or, at least, only one—to tell men again and again that I have seen the hills of Wessex as Ælfrid saw them when he overthrew the Danes.

"So the sun set. I forgot to mention that a belt of mist lay between my hill and other hills, and that it was the colour of pearl."

He broke off for the second time.

"Go on," said his mother wearily.

He shook his head.

"Go on. Nothing that you say can distress me now. I am hardened."

"I had meant to tell you the rest, but I cannot: I know that I cannot: good-bye."

Vashti stood irresolute. All her nerves were tingling with his blasphemies. But she was also inquisitive.

"This is unfair," she complained. "You have called me across the world to hear your story, and hear it I will. Tell me—as briefly as possible, for this is a disastrous waste of time—tell me how you returned to civilisation."

"Oh—that!" he said, starting. "You would like to hear about civilisation. Certainly. Had I got to where my respirator fell down?"

"No—but I understand everything now. You put on your respirator, and managed to walk along the surface of the earth to a vomitory, and there your conduct was reported to the Central Committee."

"By no means."

He passed his hand over his forehead, as if dispelling some strong impression. Then, resuming his narrative, he warmed to it again.

"My respirator fell about sunset. I had mentioned that the fountain seemed feebler, had I not."

"Yes."

"About sunset, it let the respirator fall. As I said, I had entirely forgotten about the Machine, and I paid no great attention at the time, being occupied with other things. I had my pool of air, into which I could dip when the outer keenness became intolerable, and which would possibly remain for days, provided that no wind sprang up to disperse it. Not until it was too late, did I realize what the stoppage of the escape implied. You see—the gap in the tunnel had been mended; the Mending Apparatus; the Mending Apparatus, was after me.

"One other warning I had, but I neglected it. The sky at night was clearer than it had been in the day, and the moon, which was about half the sky behind the sun, shone into the dell at moments quite brightly. I was in my usual place—on the boundary between the two atmospheres—when I thought I saw something dark move across the bottom of the dell, and vanish into the shaft. In my folly, I ran down. I bent over and listened, and I thought I heard a faint scraping noise in the depths.

"At this—but it was too late—I took alarm. I determined to put on my respirator and to walk right out of the dell. But my respirator had gone. I knew exactly where it had fallen—between the stopper and the aperture—and I could even feel the mark that it had made in the turf. It had gone, and I realized that something evil was at work, and I had better escape to the other air, and, if I must die, die running towards the cloud that had been the colour of a pearl. I never started. Out of the shaft—it is too horrible. A worm, a long white worm, had crawled out of the shaft and was gliding over the moonlit grass.

"I screamed. I did everything that I should not have done, I stamped upon the creature instead of flying from it, and it at once curled round the ankle. Then we fought. The worm let me run all over the dell, but edged up my leg as I ran. 'Help!' I cried. (That part is too awful. It belongs to the part that you will never know.) 'Help!' I cried. (Why cannot we suffer in silence?) 'Help!' I cried. Then my feet were wound together, I fell, I was dragged away from the dear ferns and the living hills, and past the great metal stopper (I can tell you this part), and I thought it might save me again if I caught hold of the handle. It also was enwrapped, it also. Oh, the whole dell was full of the things. They were searching it in all directions, they were denuding it, and the white snouts of others peeped out of the hole, ready if needed. Everything that could be moved they brought—brushwood, bundles of fern, everything, and down we all went intertwined into hell. The last things that I saw, ere the stopper closed after us, were certain stars, and I felt that a man of my sort lived in the sky. For I did fight, I fought till the very end, and it was only my head hitting against the ladder that quieted me. I woke up in this room. The worms had vanished. I was surrounded by artificial air, artificial light, artificial peace, and my friends were calling to me down speaking-tubes to know whether I had come across any new ideas lately."

Here his story ended. Discussion of it was impossible, and Vashti turned to go.

"It will end in Homelessness," she said quietly.

"I wish it would," retorted Kuno.

"The Machine has been most merciful."

"I prefer the mercy of God."

"By that superstitious phrase, do you mean that you could live in the outer air?"

"Yes."

"Have you ever seen, round the vomitories, the bones of those who were extruded after the Great Rebellion?"

"Yes."

"They were left where they perished for our edification. A few crawled away, but they perished, too—who can doubt it? And so with the Homeless of our own day. The surface of the earth supports life no longer."

"Indeed."

"Ferns and a little grass may survive, but all higher forms have perished. Has any air-ship detected them?"

"No."

"Has any lecturer dealt with them?"

"No."

"Then why this obstinacy?"

"Because I have seen them," he exploded.

"Seen *what?*"

"Because I have seen her in the twilight—because she came to my help when I called—because she, too, was entangled by the worms, and, luckier than I, was killed by one of them piercing her throat."

He was mad. Vashti departed, nor, in the troubles that followed, did she ever see his face again.

III. THE HOMELESS

During the years that followed Kuno's escapade, two important developments took place in the Machine. On the surface they were revolutionary, but in either case men's minds had been prepared beforehand, and they did but express tendencies that were latent already.

The first of these was the abolition of respirators.

Advanced thinkers, like Vashti, had always held it foolish to visit the surface of the earth. Air-ships might be necessary, but what was the good of going out for mere curiosity and crawling along for a mile or two in a terrestrial motor? The habit was vulgar and perhaps faintly improper: it was unproductive of ideas, and had no connection with the habits that really mattered. So respirators were abolished, and with them, of course, the terrestrial motors, and except for a few lecturers, who complained that they were debarred access to their subject-matter, the development was accepted quietly. Those who still wanted to know what the earth was like had after all only to listen to some gramophone, or to look into some cinematophote. And even the lecturers acquiesced when they found that a lecture on the sea was none the less stimulating when compiled out of other lectures that had already been delivered on the same subject. "Beware of first-hand ideas!" exclaimed one of the most advanced of them. "First-hand ideas do not really exist. They are but the physical impressions produced by love and fear, and on this gross foundation who could erect a philosophy? Let your ideas be second-hand, and if possible tenth-hand, for then they will be far removed from that disturbing element—direct observation. Do not learn anything about this subject of mine—the French

Revolution. Learn instead what I think that Enicharmon thought Urizen thought Gutch thought Ho-Yung thought Chi-Bo-Sing thought Lafcadio Hearn thought Carlyle thought Mirabeau said about the French Revolution. Through the medium of these eight great minds, the blood that was shed at Paris and the windows that were broken at Versailles will be clarified to an idea which you may employ most profitably in your daily lives. But be sure that the intermediates are many and varied, for in history one authority exists to counteract another. Urizen must counteract the scepticism of Ho-Yung and Enicharmon, I must myself counteract the impetuosity of Gutch. You who listen to me are in a better position to judge about the French Revolution than I am. Your descendants will be even in a better position than you, for they will learn what you think I think, and yet another intermediate will be added to the chain. And in time"—his voice rose—"there will come a generation that has got beyond facts, beyond impressions, a generation absolutely colourless, a generation

'seraphically free
From taint of personality,'

which will see the French Revolution not as it happened, nor as they would like it to have happened, but as it would have happened, had it taken place in the days of the Machine."

Tremendous applause greeted this lecture, which did but voice a feeling already latent in the minds of men—a feeling that terrestrial facts must be ignored, and that the abolition of respirators was a positive gain. It was even suggested that air-ships should be abolished too. This was not done, because air-ships had somehow worked themselves into the Machine's system. But year by year they were used less, and mentioned less by thoughtful men.

The second great development was the re-establishment of religion.

This, too, had been voiced in the celebrated lecture. No one could mistake the reverent tone in which the peroration had concluded, and it awakened a responsive echo in the heart of each. Those who had long worshipped silently, now began to talk. They described the strange feeling of peace that came over them when they handled the Book of the Machine, the pleasure that it was to repeat certain numerals out of it, however little meaning those numerals conveyed to the outward ear, the ecstasy of touching a button, however unimportant, or of ringing an electric bell, however superfluously.

"The Machine," they exclaimed, "feeds us and clothes us and houses us; through it we speak to one another, through it we see one another, in it we have our being. The Machine is the friend of ideas and the enemy of superstition: the Machine is omnipotent, eternal; blessed is the Machine." And before long this allocution was printed on the first page of the Book, and in subsequent editions the ritual swelled into a complicated system of praise and prayer. The word "religion" was sedulously avoided, and in theory the Machine was still the creation and the implement of man. But in practice all, save a few retrogrades, worshipped it as divine. Nor was it worshipped in unity. One believer would be chiefly impressed by the blue optic plates, through which he saw other believers; another by the mending apparatus, which sinful Kuno had compared to worms; another by the lifts, another by the Book. And each would pray to this or to that, and ask it to intercede for him with the Machine as a whole. Persecution— that also was present. It did not break out, for reasons that will be set forward shortly. But it was latent, and all who did not accept the minimum known as "undenominational Mechanism" lived in danger of Homelessness, which means death, as we know.

To attribute these two great developments to the Central Committee, is to take a very narrow view of civilisation. The Central Committee announced the developments, it is true, but they were no more the cause of them than were the kings of the imperialistic period the cause of war. Rather did they yield to some invincible pressure, which came no one knew whither, and which, when gratified, was succeeded by some new pressure equally invincible. To such a state of affairs it is convenient to give the name of progress. No one confessed the Machine was out of hand. Year by year it was served with increased efficiency and decreased intelligence. The better a man knew his own duties upon it, the less he understood the duties of his neighbour, and in all the world there was not one who understood the monster as a whole. Those master brains had perished. They had left full directions, it is true, and their successors had each of them mastered a portion of those directions. But Humanity, in its desire for comfort, had over-reached itself. It had exploited the riches of nature too far. Quietly and complacently, it was sinking into decadence, and progress had come to mean the progress of the Machine.

As for Vashti, her life went peacefully forward until the final disaster. She made her room dark and slept; she awoke and made the room light. She lectured and attended lectures. She exchanged ideas with her innumerable friends and believed she was growing more spiritual. At times a friend was granted Euthanasia, and left his or her room for the homelessness that is beyond all human conception. Vashti did not much mind. After an unsuccessful lecture, she would sometimes ask for Euthanasia herself. But the death-rate was not permitted to exceed the birth-rate, and the Machine had hitherto refused it to her.

The troubles began quietly, long before she was conscious of them.

One day she was astonished at receiving a message from her son. They never communicated, having nothing in common, and she had only heard indirectly that he was still alive, and had been transferred from the northern hemisphere, where he had behaved so mischievously, to the southern—indeed, to a room not far from her own.

"Does he want me to visit him?" she thought. "Never again, never. And I have not the time."

No, it was madness of another kind.

He refused to visualize his face upon the blue plate, and speaking out of the darkness with solemnity said:

"The Machine stops."

"What do you say?"

"The Machine is stopping, I know it, I know the signs."

She burst into a peal of laughter. He heard her and was angry, and they spoke no more.

"Can you imagine anything more absurd?" she cried to a friend. "A man who was my son believes that the Machine is stopping. It would be impious if it was not mad."

"The Machine is stopping?" her friend replied. "What does that mean? The phrase conveys nothing to me."

"Nor to me."

"He does not refer, I suppose, to the trouble there has been lately with the music?"

"Oh no, of course not. Let us talk about music."

"Have you complained to the authorities?"

"Yes, and they say it wants mending, and referred me to the Committee of the Mending Apparatus. I complained of those curious gasping sighs that disfigure the symphonies of the Brisbane school. They sound like some one in pain. The Committee of the Mending Apparatus say that it shall be remedied shortly."

Obscurely worried, she resumed her life. For one thing, the defect in the music irritated her. For another thing, she could not forget Kuno's speech. If he had known that the music was out of repair—he could not know it, for he detested music—if he had known that it was wrong, "the Machine stops" was exactly the venomous sort of remark he would have made. Of course he had made it at a venture, but the coincidence annoyed her, and she spoke with some petulance to the Committee of the Mending Apparatus.

They replied, as before, that the defect would be set right shortly.

"Shortly! At once!" she retorted. "Why should I be worried by imperfect music? Things are always put right at once. If you do not mend it at once, I shall complain to the Central Committee."

"No personal complaints are received by the Central Committee," the Committee of the Mending Apparatus replied.

"Through whom am I to make my complaint, then?"

"Through us."

"I complain then."

"Your complaint shall be forwarded in its turn."

"Have others complained?"

This question was unmechanical, and the Committee of the Mending Apparatus refused to answer it.

"It is too bad!" she exclaimed to another of her friends. "There never was such an unfortunate woman as myself. I can never be sure of my music now. It gets worse and worse each time I summon it."

"I too have my troubles," the friend replied. "Sometimes my ideas are interrupted by a slight jarring noise."

"What is it?"

"I do not know whether it is inside my head, or inside the wall."

"Complain, in either case."

"I have complained, and my complaint will be forwarded in its turn to the Central Committee."

Time passed, and they resented the defects no longer. The defects had not been remedied, but the human tissues in that latter day had become so subservient, that they readily adapted themselves to every caprice of the Machine. The sigh at the crisis of the Brisbane symphony no longer irritated Vashti; she accepted it as part of the melody. The jarring noise, whether in the head or in the wall, was no longer resented by her friend. And so with the mouldy artificial fruit, so with the bath water that began to stink, so with the defective rhymes that the poetry machine had taken to emit. All were bitterly complained of at first, and then acquiesced in and forgotten. Things went from bad to worse unchallenged.

It was otherwise with the failure of the sleeping apparatus. That was a more serious stoppage. There came a day when over the whole world—in Sumatra, in Wessex, in the innumerable cities of Courland and Brazil—the beds, when summoned by their tired owners, failed to appear. It may seem a ludicrous matter, but from it we may date the collapse of humanity. The Committee responsible for the failure was assailed by complainants, whom it referred, as usual, to the Committee of the Mending Apparatus, who in its turn assured them that their complaints would be forwarded to the Central Committee. But the discontent grew, for mankind was not yet sufficiently adaptable to do without sleeping.

"Some one is meddling with the Machine——" they began.

"Some one is trying to make himself king, to reintroduce the personal element."

"Punish that man with Homelessness."

"To the rescue! Avenge the Machine! Avenge the Machine!"

"War! Kill the man!"

But the Committee of the Mending Apparatus now came forward, and allayed the panic with well-chosen words. It confessed that the Mending Apparatus was itself in need of repair.

The effect of this frank confession was admirable.

"Of course," said a famous lecturer—he of the French Revolution, who gilded each new decay with splendour—"of course we shall not press our complaints now. The Mending Apparatus has treated us so well in the past that we all sympathize with it, and will wait patiently for its recovery. In its own good time it will resume its duties. Meanwhile let us do without our beds, our tabloids, our other little wants. Such, I feel sure, would be the wish of the Machine."

Thousands of miles away his audience applauded. The Machine still linked them. Under the seas, beneath the roots of the mountains, ran the wires through which they saw and heard, the enormous eyes and ears that were their heritage, and the hum of many workings clothed their thoughts in one garment of subserviency. Only the old and the sick remained ungrateful, for it was rumoured that Euthanasia, too, was out of order, and that pain had reappeared among men.

It became difficult to read. A blight entered the atmosphere and dulled its luminosity. At times Vashti could scarcely see across her room. The air, too, was foul. Loud were the complaints, impotent the remedies, heroic the tone of the lecturer as he cried: "Courage, courage! What matter so long as the Machine goes on? To it the darkness and the light are one." And though things improved again after a time, the old brilliancy was never recaptured, and humanity never recovered from its entrance into twilight. There was an hysterical talk of "measures," of "provisional dictatorship," and the inhabitants of Sumatra were asked to familiarize themselves with the workings of the central power station, the said power station being situated in France. But for the most part panic reigned, and men spent their strength praying to their Books, tangible proofs of the Machine's omnipotence. There were gradations of terror—at times came rumours of hope—the Mending Apparatus was almost mended—the enemies of the Machine had been got under—new "nerve-centres" were evolving which would do the work even more magnificently than before. But there came a day when, without the slightest warning, without any previous hint of feebleness, the entire communication-system broke down, all over the world, and the world, as they understood it, ended.

Vashti was lecturing at the time and her earlier remarks had been punctuated with applause. As she proceeded the audience became silent, and at the conclusion there was no sound. Somewhat displeased, she called to a friend who was a specialist in sympathy. No sound: doubtless the friend was sleeping. And so with the next friend whom she tried to summon, and so with the next, until she remembered Kuno's cryptic remark, "The Machine stops."

The phrase still conveyed nothing. If Eternity was stopping it would of course be set going shortly.

For example, there was still a little light and air—the atmosphere had improved a few hours previously. There was still the Book, and while there was the Book there was security.

Then she broke down, for with the cessation of activity came an unexpected terror—silence.

She had never known silence, and the coming of it nearly killed her—it did kill many thousands of people outright. Ever since her birth she had been surrounded by the steady hum. It was to the ear what artificial air was to the lungs, and agonizing pains shot across her head. And scarcely knowing what she did, she stumbled forward and pressed the unfamiliar button, the one that opened the door of her cell.

Now the door of the cell worked on a simple hinge of its own. It was not connected with the central power station, dying far away in France. It opened, rousing immoderate hopes in Vashti, for she thought that the Machine had been mended. It opened, and she saw the dim tunnel that curved far away towards freedom. One look, and then she shrank back. For the tunnel was full of people—she was almost the last in that city to have taken alarm.

People at any time repelled her, and these were nightmares from her worst dreams. People were crawling about, people were screaming, whimpering, gasping for breath, touching each other, vanishing in the dark, and ever and anon being pushed off the platform on to the live rail. Some were fighting round the electric bells, trying to summon trains which could not be summoned. Others were yelling for Euthanasia or for respirators, or blaspheming the Machine. Others stood at the doors of their cells fearing, like herself, either to stop in them or to leave them. And behind all the uproar was silence—the silence which is the voice of the earth and of the generations who have gone.

No—it was worse than solitude. She closed the door again and sat down to wait for the end. The disintegration went on, accompanied by horrible cracks and rumbling. The valves that restrained the Medical Apparatus must have been weakened, for it ruptured and hung hideously from the ceiling. The floor heaved and fell and flung her from her chair. A tube oozed towards her serpent fashion. And at last the final horror approached—light began to ebb, and she knew that civilisation's long day was closing.

She whirled round, praying to be saved from this, at any rate, kissing the Book, pressing button after button. The uproar outside was increasing, and even penetrated the wall. Slowly the brilliancy of her cell was dimmed, the reflections faded from her metal switches. Now she could not see the reading-stand, now not the Book, though she held it in her hand. Light followed the flight of sound, air was following light, and the original void returned to the cavern from which it had been so long excluded. Vashti continued to whirl, like the devotees of an earlier religion, screaming, praying, striking at the buttons with bleeding hands.

It was thus that she opened her prison and escaped —escaped in the spirit: at least so it seems to me, ere my meditation closes. That she escapes in the body —I cannot perceive that. She struck, by chance, the switch that released the door, and the rush of foul air on her skin, the loud throbbing whispers in her ears, told her that she was facing the tunnel again, and that tremendous platform on which she had seen men fighting. They were not fighting now. Only the whispers remained, and the little whimpering groans. They were dying by hundreds out in the dark.

She burst into tears.

Tears answered her.

They wept for humanity, those two, not for themselves. They could not bear that this should be the end. Ere silence was completed their hearts were opened, and they knew what had been important on the earth. Man, the flower of all flesh, the noblest of all creatures visible, man who had once made god in his image, and had mirrored his strength on the constellations, beautiful naked man was dying, strangled in the garments that he had woven. Century after century had he toiled, and here was his reward. Truly the garment had seemed heavenly at first, shot with the colours of culture, sewn with the threads of self-denial. And heavenly it had been so long as it was a garment and no more, so long as man could shed it at will and live by the essence that is his soul, and the essence, equally divine, that is his body. The sin against the body—it was for that they wept in chief; the centuries of wrong against the muscles and the nerves, and those five portals by which we can alone apprehend—glozing it over with talk of evolution, until the body was white pap, the home of ideas as colourless, last sloshy stirrings of a spirit that had grasped the stars.

"Where are you?" she sobbed.

His voice in the darkness said, "Here."

"Is there any hope, Kuno?"

"None for us."

"Where are you?"

She crawled towards him over the bodies of the dead. His blood spurted over her hands.

"Quicker," he gasped, "I am dying—but we touch, we talk, not through the Machine."

He kissed her.

"We have come back to our own. We die, but we have recaptured life, as it was in Wessex, when Ælfrid overthrew the Danes. We know what they know outside, they who dwelt in the cloud that is the colour of a pearl."

"But, Kuno, is it true? Are there still men on the surface of the earth? Is this—this tunnel, this poisoned darkness—really not the end?"

He replied:

"I have seen them, spoken to them, loved them. They are hiding in the mist and the ferns until our civilisation stops. Today they are the Homeless—tomorrow——"

"Oh, tomorrow—some fool will start the Machine again, tomorrow."

"Never," said Kuno, "never. Humanity has learnt its lesson."

As he spoke, the whole city was broken like a honeycomb. An air-ship had sailed in through the vomitory into a ruined wharf. It crashed downwards, exploding as it went, rending gallery after gallery with its wings of steel. For a moment they saw the nations of the dead, and, before they joined them, scraps of the untainted sky.

THE NATURE THEATRE
OF OKLAHOMA

Franz Kafka

AT A STREET CORNER Karl saw a placard with the following announcement: The Oklahoma Theatre will engage members for its company today at Clayton race-course from six o'clock in the morning until midnight. The great Theatre of Oklahoma calls you! Today only and never again! If you miss your chance now you miss it for ever! If you think of your future you are one of us! Everyone is welcome! If you want to be an artist, join our company! Our Theatre can find employment for everyone, a place for everyone! If you decide on an engagement we congratulate you here and now! But hurry, so that you get in before midnight! At twelve o'clock the doors will be shut and never opened again! Down with all those who do not believe in us! Up, and to Clayton!

A great many people were certainly standing before the placard, but it did not seem to find much
approval. There were so many placards; nobody believed in them any longer. And this placard was still
more improbable than usual. Above all, it failed in
an essential particular, it did not mention payment.
If the payment were worth mentioning at all, the
placard would certainly have mentioned it; that
most attractive of all arguments would not have
been forgotten. No one wanted to be an artist, but
every man wanted to be paid for his labours.

Yet for Karl there was one great attraction in the
placard. "Everyone is welcome," it said. Everyone,
that meant Karl too. All that he had done till now
was ignored; it was not going to be made a reproach
to him. He was entitled to apply for a job of which
he need not be ashamed, which, on the contrary,
was a matter of public advertisement. And just as
public was the promise that he too would find acceptance. He asked for nothing better; he wanted to
find some way of at least beginning a decent life, and
perhaps this was his chance. Even if all the extrava-
gant statements in the placard were a lie, even if the
great Theatre of Oklahoma were an insignificant

travelling circus, it wanted to engage people, and that was enough. Karl did not read the whole placard over again, but once more singled out the sentence: "Everyone is welcome." At first he thought of going to Clayton on foot; yet that would mean three hours of hard walking, and in all possibility he might arrive just in time to hear that every available vacancy had been filled. The placard certainly suggested that there were no limits to the number of people who could be engaged, but all advertisements of that kind were worded like that. Karl saw that he must either give it up or else go by train. He counted over his money, which would last him for eight days yet if he did not take this railway journey; he slid the little coins backwards and forwards on the palm of his hand. A gentleman who had been watching him clapped him on the shoulder and said: "All good luck for your journey to Clayton." Karl nodded silently and reckoned up his money again. But he soon came to a decision, counted out the money he needed for the fare and rushed to the underground station. When he got out at Clayton he heard at once the noise of many trumpets. It was a confused blaring; the trumpets were not in harmony but were blown regardless of each other. Still, that did not worry Karl; he took it rather as a confirmation of the fact that the Theatre of Oklahoma was a great undertaking. But when he emerged from the station and surveyed the lay-out before him, he realised that it was all on a much larger scale than he could have conceived possible, and he did not understand how any organisation could make such extensive preparations merely for the purpose of taking on employees. Before the entrance to the race-course a long low platform had been set up, on which hundreds of women dressed as angels in white robes with great wings on their shoulders were blowing on long trumpets that glittered like gold. They were not actually standing on the platform, but were mounted on separate pedestals, which could not however be seen, since they were completely hidden by the long flowing draperies of the robes. Now, as the pedestals were very high, some of them quite six feet high, these women looked gigantic, except that the smallness of their heads spoiled a little the impression of size, and their loose hair looked too short and almost absurd hanging between the great wings and framing their faces. To avoid monotony, the pedestals were of all sizes; there were women quite low down, not much over life-size, but beside them others soared to such a height that one felt the slightest gust of wind could capsize them. And all these women were blowing their trumpets.

There were not many listeners. Dwarfed by comparison with these great figures, some ten boys were walking about before the platform and looking up at the women. They called each other's attention to this one or that, but seemed to have no idea of entering and offering their services. Only one older man was to be seen; he stood a little to one side. He had brought his wife with him and a child in a perambulator. The wife was holding the perambulator with one hand and with the other supporting herself on her husband's shoulder. They were clearly admiring the spectacle, but one could see all the same that they were disappointed. They too had apparently expected to find some sign of work, and this blowing of trumpets confused them. Karl was in the same position. He walked over to where the man was standing, listened for a little to the trumpets, and then said: "Isn't this the place where they are engaging people for the Theatre of Oklahoma?"

"I thought so too," said the man, "but we've been waiting here for an hour and heard nothing but these trumpets. There's not a placard to be seen, no announcers, nobody anywhere to tell you what to do."

Karl said: "Perhaps they're waiting until more people arrive. There are really very few here."

"Possibly," said the man, and they were silent again. Besides, it was difficult to hear anything through the din of the trumpets. But then the woman whispered to her husband; he nodded and she called at once to Karl: "Couldn't you go into the race-course and ask where the workers are being taken on?"

"Yes," said Karl, "but I would have to cross the platform, among all the angels."

"Is that so very difficult?" asked the woman.

She seemed to think it an easy path for Karl, but she was unwilling to let her husband go.

"All right," said Karl, "I'll go."

"That's very good of you," said the woman, and both she and her husband took Karl's hand and pressed it.

The boys all came rushing up to get a near view of

Karl climbing the platform. It was as if the women redoubled their efforts on the trumpets as a greeting to the first applicant. Those whose pedestals Karl had to pass actually took their trumpets from their mouths and leaned over to follow him with their eyes. At the other side of the platform Karl discovered a man walking restlessly up and down, obviously only waiting for people so as to give them all the information they might desire. Karl was just about to accost him, when he heard someone calling his name above him.

"Karl!" cried an angel. Karl looked up and in delighted surprise began to laugh. It was Fanny.

"Fanny!" he exclaimed, waving his hand.

"Come up here!" cried Fanny. "You're surely not going to pass me like that!" And she parted her draperies so that the pedestal and a little ladder leading up to it became visible.

"Is one allowed to go up?" asked Karl.

"Who can forbid us to shake hands!" cried Fanny, and she looked round indignantly, in case anyone might be coming to intervene. But Karl was already running up the ladder.

"Not so fast!" cried Fanny. "The pedestal and

both of us will come to grief!" But nothing happened, Karl reached the top in safety. "Just look," said Fanny after they had greeted each other, "just look what a job I've got."

"It's a fine job," said Karl, looking round him. All the women near by had noticed him and began to giggle. "You're almost the highest of them all," said Karl, and he stretched out his hand to measure the height of the others.

"I saw you at once," said Fanny, "as soon as you came out of the station, but I'm in the last row here, unfortunately, nobody can see me, and I couldn't shout either. I blew as loudly as I could, but you didn't recognise me."

"You all play very badly," said Karl, "let me have a turn."

"Why, certainly," said Fanny, handing him the trumpet, "but don't spoil the show, or else I'll get the sack."

Karl began to blow into the trumpet; he had imagined it was a roughly-fashioned trumpet intended merely to make a noise, but now he discovered that it was an instrument capable of almost any refinement of expression. If all the instruments were of the same quality, they were being very ill-used. Paying no attention to the blaring of the others he played with all the power of his lungs an air which he had once heard in some tavern or other. He felt happy at having found an old friend, and at being allowed to play a trumpet as a special privilege, and at the thought that he might likely get a good post very soon. Many of the women stopped playing to listen; when he suddenly broke off scarcely half of the trumpets were in action; and it took a little while for the general din to work up to full power again.

"But you are an artist," said Fanny, when Karl handed her the trumpet again. "Ask to be taken on as a trumpeter."

"Are men taken on for it too?" asked Karl.

"Oh yes," said Fanny. "We play for two hours; then we're relieved by men who are dressed as devils. Half of them blow, the other half beat on drums. It's very fine, but the whole outfit is just as lavish. Don't you think our robes are beautiful? And the wings?" she looked down at herself.

"Do you think," asked Karl, "that I'll get a job here too?"

"Most certainly," said Fanny, "why, it's the greatest theatre in the world. What a piece of luck that we're to be together again. All the same, it depends on what job you get. For it would be quite possible for us not to see each other at all, even though we were both engaged here."

"Is the place really so big as that?" asked Karl.

"It's the biggest theatre in the world," Fanny said again, "I haven't seen it yet myself, I admit, but some of the other girls here, who have been in Oklahoma already, say that there are almost no limits to it."

"But there aren't many people here," said Karl, pointing down at the boys and the little family.

"That's true," said Fanny. "But consider that we pick up people in all the towns, that our recruiting outfit here is always on the road, and that there are ever so many of these outfits."

"Why, has the theatre not opened yet?" asked Karl.

"Oh yes," said Fanny, "it's an old theatre, but it is always being enlarged."

"I'm surprised," said Karl, "that more people don't flock to join it."

"Yes," said Fanny, "it's extraordinary."

"Perhaps," said Karl, "this display of angels and devils frightens people off more than it attracts them."

"What made you think of that?" said Fanny. "But you may be right. Tell that to our leader; perhaps it might be helpful."

"Where is he?" asked Karl.

"On the race-course," said Fanny, "on the umpire's platform."

"That surprises me too," said Karl, "why a race-course for engaging people?"

"Oh," said Fanny, "we always make great preparations in case there should be a great crowd. There's lots of space on a race-course. And in all the stands where the bets are laid on ordinary days, offices are set up to sign on recruits. There must be two hundred different offices there."

"But," cried Karl, "has the Theatre of Oklahoma such a huge income that it can maintain recruiting establishments to that extent?"

"What does that matter to us?" said Fanny. "But you'd better go now, Karl, so that you don't miss anything; and I must begin to blow my trumpet again. Do your best to get a job in this outfit, and come and tell me at once. Remember that I'll be waiting very impatiently for the news."

She pressed his hand, warned him to be cautious in climbing down, set the trumpet to her lips again, but did not blow it until she saw Karl safely on the ground. Karl arranged the robe over the ladder again, as it had been before, Fanny nodded her thanks, and Karl, still considering from various angles what he had just heard, approached the man, who had already seen him up on Fanny's pedestal and had come close to it to wait for him.

"You want to join us?" asked the man. "I am the staff manager of this company and I bid you welcome." He had a slight permanent stoop as if out of politeness, fidgeted with his feet, though without moving from the spot, and played with his watch chain.

"Thank you," said Karl, "I read the placard your company put out and I have come here as I was requested."

"Quite right," said the man appreciatively. "Unluckily there aren't many who do the same." It occurred to Karl that he could now tell the man that perhaps the recruiting company failed because of the very splendour of its attractions. But he did not say so, for this man was not the leader of the company, and besides it would not be much of a recommendation for him if he began to make suggestions for the improvement of the outfit before even being taken on. So he merely said: "There is another man waiting out there who wants to report here too and simply sent me on ahead. May I fetch him now?"

"Of course," said the man, "the more the better."

"He has a wife with him too and a small child in a perambulator. Are they to come too?"

"Of course," said the man, and he seemed to smile at Karl's doubts. "We can use all of them."

"I'll be back in a minute," said Karl, and he ran back to the edge of the platform. He waved to the married couple and shouted that everybody could come. He helped the man to lift the perambulator on to the platform, and then they proceeded together. The boys, seeing this, consulted with each other, and then, their hands in their pockets, hesitating to the last instant, slowly climbed on to the platform and followed Karl and the family. Just then some fresh passengers emerged from the underground station and raised their arms in astonishment when they saw the platform and the angels. However, it seemed that the competition for jobs would now become more lively. Karl felt very glad that he was such an early arrival, perhaps the first of them all; the married couple were apprehensive and asked various questions as to whether great demands would be made on them. Karl told them he knew nothing definite yet, but he had received the impression that everyone without exception would be engaged. He thought they could feel easy in their minds. The staff manager advanced towards them, very satisfied that so many were coming; he rubbed his hands, greeted everyone with a little bow and arranged them all in a row. Karl was the first, then came the husband and wife, and after that the others. When they were all ranged up—the boys kept jostling each other at first and it took some time to get them in order—the staff manager said, while the trumpets fell silent: "I greet you in the name of the Theatre of Oklahoma. You have come early," (but it was already midday), "there is no great rush yet, so that the formalities necessary for engaging you will soon be settled. Of course you have all your identification papers."

The boys at once pulled papers out of their pockets and flourished them at the staff manager; the husband nudged his wife, who pulled out a whole bundle of papers from under the blankets of the perambulator. But Karl had none. Would that prevent him from being taken on? He knew well enough from experience that with a little resolution it should be easy to get round such regulations. Very likely he would succeed. The staff manager glanced along the row, assured himself that everyone had papers, and since Karl also stood with his hand raised, though it was empty, he assumed that in his case too everything was in order.

"Very good," said the staff manager, with a reassuring wave of the hand to the boys, who wanted to have their papers examined at once, "the papers will now be scrutinised in the employment bureaus. As you will have seen already from our placard, we can find employment for everyone. But we must know of course what occupations you have followed until now, so that we can put you in the right places to make use of your knowledge."

"But it's a theatre," thought Karl dubiously, and he listened very intently.

"We have accordingly," went on the staff manager, "set up employment bureaus in the bookmakers' booths, an office for each trade or profession. So each of you will now tell me his occupation; a family is generally registered at the husband's employment bureau. I shall then take you to the offices, where first your papers and then your qualifications will be checked by experts; it will only be a quite short examination; there's nothing to be afraid of. You will then be signed on at once and receive your further instructions. So let us begin. This first office is for engineers, as the inscription tells you. Is there perhaps an engineer here?"

Karl stepped forward. He thought that his lack of papers made it imperative for him to rush through the formalities with all possible speed; he had also a slight justification in putting himself forward, for he had once wanted to be an engineer. But when the boys saw Karl reporting himself they grew envious and put up their hands too, all of them. The staff manager rose to his full height and said to the boys: "Are you engineers?" Their hands slowly wavered and sank, but Karl stuck to his first decision. The staff manager certainly looked at him with incredulity, for Karl seemed too wretchedly clad and also too young to be an engineer; but he said nothing further, perhaps out of gratitude because Karl, at least in his opinion, had brought the applicants in. He simply pointed courteously towards the office, and Karl went across to it, while the staff manager turned to the others.

In the bureau for engineers two gentlemen were sitting at either side of a rectangular counter comparing two big lists which lay before them. One of them read while the other made a mark against names in his list. When Karl appeared and greeted them, they laid aside the lists at once and brought out two great books, which they flung open.

One of them, who was obviously only a clerk, said: "Please give me your identity papers."

"I am sorry to say I haven't got them with me," said Karl.

"He hasn't got them with him," said the clerk to the other gentleman, at once writing down the answer in his book.

"You are an engineer?" thereupon asked the other man, who seemed to be in charge of the bureau.

"I'm not an engineer yet," said Karl quickly, "but——"

"Enough," said the gentleman still more quickly, "in that case you don't belong to us. Be so good as to note the inscription." Karl clenched his teeth, and the gentleman must have observed that, for he said: "There's no need to worry. We can employ everyone." And he made a sign to one of the attendants who were lounging about idly between the barriers: "Lead this gentleman to the bureau for technicians."

The attendant interpreted the command literally and took Karl by the hand. They passed a number of booths on either side; in one Karl saw one of the boys, who had already been signed on and was gratefully shaking hands with the gentleman in charge. In the bureau to which Karl was now taken the procedure was similar to that in the first office, as he had foreseen. Except that they now despatched him to the bureau for intermediate pupils, when they heard that he had attended an intermediate school. But when Karl confessed there that it was a European school he had attended, the officials refused to accept him and had him conducted to the bureau for European intermediate pupils. It was a booth on the outer verge of the course, not only smaller but also humbler than all the others. The attendant who conducted him there was furious at the long pilgrimage and the repeated rebuffs, for which in his opinion Karl alone bore the blame. He did not wait for the questioning to begin, but went away at once. So this bureau was probably Karl's last chance. When Karl caught sight of the head of the bureau, he was almost startled at his close resemblance to a teacher who was presumably still teaching in the school at home. The resemblance, however, as immediately appeared, was confined to certain details; but the spectacles resting on the man's broad nose, the fair beard as carefully tended as a prize exhibit, the slightly rounded back and the unexpectedly loud abrupt voice held Karl in amazement for some time. Fortunately, he had not to attend very carefully, for the procedure here was much simpler than in the other offices. A note was certainly taken of the fact that his papers were lacking, and the head of the bureau called it an incomprehensible piece of negligence; but the clerk, who seemed to have the upper hand, quickly glossed it over and after a few brief questions by his superior, while that gentleman was just preparing to put some more important ones, he declared that Karl had been engaged. The head of the bureau turned with open mouth upon his clerk, but the clerk made a definitive gesture with his hand, said: "Engaged," and at once entered the decision in his book. Obviously the clerk considered a European intermediate pupil to be something so ignominious that anyone who admitted to being one was not worth disbelieving. Karl for his part had no objection to this; he went up to the clerk intending to thank him. But there was another little delay, while they asked him what his name was. He did not reply at once; he felt shy of mentioning his own name and letting it be written down. As soon as he had a place here, no matter how small, and filled it satisfactorily, they could have his name, but not now; he had concealed it too long to give it away now. So as no other name occurred to him at the moment, he gave the nickname he had had in his last post: "Negro."

"Negro?" said the chief, turning his head and making a grimace, as if Karl had now touched the high water mark of incredibility. Even the clerk looked critically at Karl for a while, but then he said: "Negro" and wrote the name down.

"But you surely haven't written down Negro?" his chief shouted at him.

"Yes, Negro," said the clerk calmly, and waved his hand, as if his superior should now continue the proceedings. And the head of the bureau, controlling himself, stood up and said: "You are engaged, then, for the——" but he could not get any farther, he could not go against his own conscience, so he sat down and said: "He isn't called Negro."

The clerk raised his eyebrows, got up himself and said: "Then it is my duty to inform you that you have been engaged for the Theatre in Oklahoma and that you will now be introduced to our leader."

Another attendant was summoned, who conducted Karl to the umpire's platform.

At the foot of the steps Karl caught sight of the perambulator, and at that moment the father and mother descended, the mother with the baby on her arm.

"Have you been taken on?" asked the man; he was much more lively than before, and his wife smiled at Karl across her shoulder. When Karl answered that he had just been taken on and was going to be introduced, the man said: "Then I congratulate you. We have been taken on too. It seems to be a good thing, though you can't get used to everything all at once; but it's like that everywhere."

They said goodbye to each other again and Karl climbed up to the platform. He took his time, for the small space above seemed to be crammed with people, and he did not want to be importunate. He even paused for a while and gazed at the great race-course, which extended on every side to distant woods. He was filled with longing to see a horse-race; he had found no opportunity to do so since he had come to America. In Europe he had once been taken to a race-meeting as a small child, but all that he could remember was that he had been dragged by his mother through throngs of people who were unwilling to make room and let him pass. So that actually he had never seen a race yet. Behind him a mechanism of some kind began to whir; he turned round and saw on the board, where the names of the winners appeared, the following inscription being hoisted: "The merchant Kala with wife and child." So the names of those who were engaged were communicated to all the offices from here.

At that moment several gentlemen with pencils

and notebooks in their hands ran down the stairs, busily talking to each other; Karl squeezed against the railing to let them pass, and then went up, as there was now room for him above. In one corner of the platform with its wooden railing—the whole looked like the flat roof of a small tower—a gentleman was sitting with his arms stretched along the railing and a broad white silk sash hanging diagonally across his chest with the inscription: "Leader of the tenth recruiting squad of the Theatre of Oklahoma." On a table stood a telephone, doubtless installed for use during the races but now obviously employed in giving the leader all necessary information regarding the various applicants before they were introduced, for he did not begin by putting questions to Karl, but said to a gentleman sitting beside him with crossed legs, his chin in his hands: "Negro, a European intermediate pupil." And as if with that he had nothing more to say to Karl, who was bowing low before him, he glanced down the stairs to see whether anyone else was coming. As no one came, he lent an ear to the conversation which the other gentleman was having with Karl, but for the most part kept looking at the race-course and tapping on the railing with his fingers. These delicate and yet powerful, long and nimble fingers attracted Karl's attention from time to time, although he should really have been giving his whole mind to the other gentleman.

"You've been out of work?" this gentleman began by asking. The question, like almost all the other questions he asked, was very simple and direct, nor did he check Karl's replies by cross-examining him at all; yet the way in which he rounded his eyes while he uttered his questions, the way in which he leaned forward to contemplate their effect, the way in which he let his head sink to his chest while he listened to the replies, in some cases repeating them aloud, invested his enquiries with an air of special significance, which one might not understand but which it made one uneasy to suspect. Many times Karl felt impelled to take back the answer he had given and substitute another which might find more approval, but he always managed to refrain, for he knew what a bad impression such shilly-shallying was bound to make, and how little he really understood for the most part the effect of his answers. Besides, his engagement seemed to be already decided upon, and the consciousness of that gave him support.

To the question whether he had been out of work he replied with a simple "Yes."

"Where were you engaged last?" the gentleman asked next.

Karl was just about to answer, when the gentleman raised his first finger and repeated again: "Last!"

As Karl had understood the question perfectly well, he involuntarily shook his head to reject the confusing additional remark and answered: "In an office."

That was the truth, but if the gentleman should demand more definite information regarding the kind of office, he would have to tell lies. However, the necessity did not arise, for the gentleman asked a question which it was quite easy to answer with perfect truth: "Were you satisfied there?"

"No!" exclaimed Karl, almost before the question was finished. Out of the corner of his eye he could see that the leader was smiling faintly. He regretted the impetuosity of his exclamation, but it was too tempting to launch that no, for during all his last term of service his greatest wish had been that some outside employer of labour might come in and ask him that very question. Still, his negative might put him at another disadvantage if the gentleman were to follow it up by asking why he had not been satisfied? But he asked instead: "For what kind of post do you feel you are best suited?" This question might contain a real trap, for why was it put at all since he had already been engaged as an actor? But although he saw the difficulty, he could not bring himself to say that he felt particularly suited for the acting profession. So he evaded the question and said, at the risk of appearing obstructive: "I read the placard in the town, and as it said there that you could employ anyone, I came here."

"We know that," said the gentleman, showing by his ensuing silence that he insisted on an answer to the question.

"I have been engaged as an actor," said Karl hesitantly, to let the gentleman see that he found himself in a dilemma.

"Quite so," said the gentleman, and fell silent again.

"No," said Karl, and all his hopes of being settled in a job began to totter, "I don't know whether I'm capable of being an actor. But I shall do my best and try to carry out all my instructions."

The gentleman turned to the leader, both of them nodded; Karl seemed to have given the right answer, so he took courage again and standing erect waited for the next question: It ran: "What did you want to study originally?"

To define the question more exactly—the gentleman seemed to lay great weight on exact definition, —he added: "In Europe, I mean," at the same time removing his hand from his chin and waving it slightly as if to indicate both how remote Europe was and how unimportant were any plans that might have been made there.

Karl said: "I wanted to be an engineer." This answer almost stuck in his throat; it was absurd of him, knowing as he did the kind of career he had had in America, to bring up the old day-dream of having wanted to be an engineer—would he ever have become an engineer even in Europe?—but he simply did not know what other answer to make and so gave this one.

Yet the gentleman took it seriously, as he took everything seriously. "Well, you can't turn into an engineer all at once," he said, "but perhaps it would suit you for the time being to be attached to some minor technical work."

"Certainly," said Karl. He was perfectly satisfied; true, if he accepted the offer, he would be transferred from the acting profession to the lower status of technical labourer, but he really believed that he would be able to do more justice to himself at technical work. Besides, he kept on telling himself, it was not so much a matter of the kind of work as of establishing oneself permanently somewhere.

"Are you strong enough for heavy work?" asked the gentleman.

"Oh yes," said Karl.

At that, the gentleman asked Karl to come nearer and felt his arm.

"He's a strong lad," he said, then pulling Karl by the arm towards the leader. The leader nodded smilingly, reached Karl his hand without changing his lazy posture, and said: "Then that's all settled. In Oklahoma we'll look into it again. See that you do honour to our recruiting squad!"

Karl made his bow, and also turned to say good-bye to the other gentleman, but he, as if his functions were now discharged, was walking up and down the platform gazing at the sky. As Karl went down the steps, the announcement board beside them was showing the inscription: "Negro, technical worker."

As everything here was taking an orderly course, Karl felt that after all he would not have minded seeing his real name on the board. The organisation was indeed scrupulously precise, for at the foot of the steps Karl found a waiting attendant who fastened a band round his arm. When Karl lifted his arm to see what was written on the band, there, right enough, were the words "technical worker."

But wherever he was to be taken now, he decided that he must first report to Fanny how well everything had gone. To his great sorrow he learned from the attendant that both the angels and the devils had already left for the next town on the recruiting squad's itinerary, to act as advance agents for the arrival of the troop next day.

"What a pity," said Karl; it was the first disappointment that he had had in this new undertaking, "I had a friend among the angels."

"You'll see her again in Oklahoma," said the attendant, "but now come along; you're the last."

He led Karl along the inner side of the platform on which the angels had been posted; there was nothing left but the empty pedestals. Yet Karl's assumption that if the trumpeting were stopped more people would be encouraged to apply was proved wrong, for there were now no grown-up people at all before the platform, only a few children fighting over a long, white feather which had apparently fallen out of an angel's wing. A boy was holding it up in the air, while the other children were trying to push down his head with one hand and reaching for the feather with the other.

Karl pointed out the children, but the attendant said without looking: "Come on, hurry up, it's taken a long time for you to get engaged. I suppose they weren't sure of you?"

"I don't know," said Karl in astonishment, but he did not believe it. Always, even in the most unambiguous circumstances, someone could be found to take pleasure in suggesting troubles to his fellow men. But at the friendly aspect of the Grand Stand which they were now approaching, Karl soon forgot the attendant's remark. For on this stand there was a long wide bench covered with a white cloth; all the applicants who had been taken on sat on the bench below it with their backs to the race-course and were being fed. They were all happy and excited; just as Karl, coming last, quietly took his seat several of them were rising with upraised glasses, and one of them toasted the leader of the tenth recruiting squad, whom he called the "father of all the unemployed." Someone then remarked that the leader could be seen from here, and actually the umpire's platform with the two gentlemen on it was visible at no very great distance. Now they were all raising their glasses in that direction, Karl too seized the glass standing in front of him, but loudly as they shouted and hard as they tried to draw attention to themselves, there was no sign on the umpire's platform that the ovation had been observed or at least that there was any wish to observe it. The leader lounged in his corner as before, and the other gentleman stood beside him, resting his chin on his hand. Somewhat disappointed, everybody sat down again; here and there one would turn round towards the umpire's platform again; but soon they were all well occupied with the abundant food; huge birds such as Karl had never seen before were carried round with many forks sticking into the crisply roasted meat; the glasses were kept filled with wine by the attendants—you hardly noticed it, you were busy with your plate and a stream of red wine simply fell into your glass—and those who did not want to take part in the general conversation could look at views of the Theatre of Oklahoma which lay in a pile at one end of the table and were supposed to pass from hand to hand. But few of the people troubled much about the views, and so it happened that only one of them reached Karl, who was the last in the row. Yet to judge from that picture, all the rest must have been well worth seeing. The picture showed the box reserved in the Theatre for the President of the United States. At first glance one might have thought that it was not a stage box but the stage itself, so far-flung was the sweep of its breastwork. This breastwork was made entirely of gold, to the smallest detail. Between its slender columns, as delicately carved as if cut out by a fine pair of scissors, medallions of former Presidents were arrayed side by side; one of these had a remarkably straight nose, curling lips and a downward-looking eye hooded beneath a full, rounded eye-lid. Rays of light fell into the box from all sides and from the roof; the foreground was literally bathed in light, white but soft, while the recess of the background, behind red damask curtains falling in changing folds from roof to floor and looped with cords, appeared like a duskily-glowing empty cavern. One could scarcely imagine human figures in that box, so royal did it look. Karl was not quite rapt away from his dinner, but he laid the photograph beside his plate and sat gazing at it. He would have been glad to look at even one of the other photographs, but he did not want to rise and pick one up himself, since an attendant had his hand resting on the pile and the sequence probably had to be kept unbroken; so he only craned his neck to survey the table, trying to make out if another photograph were being passed along. To his great amazement—it seemed at first incredible—he recognised among those most intent upon their plates a face which he knew well: Giacomo. At once he rose and hastened up to him. "Giacomo!" he cried.

Shy as ever when taken by surprise, Giacomo got up from his seat, turned round in the narrow space between the benches, wiped his mouth with his hand and then showed great delight at seeing Karl, suggesting that Karl should come and sit beside him, or he should change his own place instead; they had a lot to tell each other and should stick together all the time. Karl, not wanting to disturb the others, said perhaps they had better keep their own places for the time being, the meal would soon be finished and then of course they would stick together. But Karl still lingered a moment or two, only for the sake of looking at Giacomo. What memories of the past were recalled! What had happened to the Manageress? What was Therese doing? Giacomo himself had hardly changed at all in appearance; the Manageress's prophecy that in six months' time he would develop into a large-boned American had not been fulfilled; he was as delicate looking as before, his cheeks hollow as ever, though at the moment they were bulging with an extra large mouthful of meat from which he was slowly extracting the bones, to lay them on his plate. As Karl could see from his arm-band, he was not engaged as an actor either, but as a lift-boy; the Theatre of Oklahoma really did seem to have a place for everyone! But Karl's absorption in Giacomo had kept him too long away from his own seat. Just as he was thinking of getting back, the Staff Manager arrived, climbed on to one of the upper benches, clapped his hands and made a short speech while most of the people rose to their feet, those who remained in their seats, unwilling to leave their dinners, being nudged by the others until they too were forced to rise.

"I hope," said the Staff Manager, Karl meanwhile having tip-toed back to his place, "that you have been satisfied with our reception of you and the dinner we have given you. The recruiting squad is generally supposed to keep a good kitchen. I'm sorry we must clear the table already, but the train for Oklahoma is going to leave in five minutes. It's a long journey, I know, but you'll find yourselves well looked after. Let me now introduce the gentleman in charge of your transport arrangements, whose instructions you will please follow."

A lean little man scrambled up on the bench beside the Staff Manager and, scarcely taking time to make a hasty bow, began waving his arms nervously to direct them how to assemble themselves in an orderly manner and proceed to the station. But he was at first ignored, for the man who had made a speech at the beginning of the dinner now struck the table with his hand and began to return thanks in a lengthy oration, although—Karl was growing quite uneasy about it—he had just been told that the train was leaving in five minutes. He was not even deterred by the patent inattention of the Staff Manager, who was giving various instructions to the transport official; he built up his oration in the grand manner, mentioning each dish that had been served and passing a judgement on each individually, winding up with the declaration: "Gentlemen, that is the way to our hearts!" Everyone laughed except the gentlemen he was addressing, but there was more truth than jest in his statement, all the same.

This oration brought its own penalty, since the road to the station had now to be taken at a run. Still, that was no great hardship, for—as Karl only now remarked—no one carried any luggage; the only thing that could be called luggage was the perambulator, which the father was pushing at the head of the troop and which jolted up and down wildly as if no hand were steadying it. What destitute, disreputable characters were here assembled, and yet how well they had been received and cared for! And the transport official must have been told to cherish them like the apple of his eye. Now he was taking a turn at pushing the perambulator, waving one hand to encourage the troop; now he was urging on stragglers in the rear; now he was careering along the ranks, keeping an eye on the slower runners in the middle and trying to show them with swinging arms how to run more easily.

When they reached the station the train was ready for departure. People in the station pointed out the newcomers to each other, and one heard exclamations such as: "All these belong to the Theatre of Oklahoma!" The Theatre seemed to be much better known than Karl had assumed; of course, he had never taken much interest in theatrical affairs. A whole carriage was specially reserved for their troop; the transport official worked harder than the guard at getting the people into it. Only when he had inspected each compartment and made a few rearrangements did he get into his own seat. Karl had happened to get a window-seat, with Giacomo beside him. So there they sat, the two of them, close together, rejoicing in their hearts over the journey.

Such a carefree journey in America they had never known. When the train began to move out of the station they waved from the window, to the amusement of the young men opposite, who nudged each other and laughed.

For two days and two nights they journeyed on. Only now did Karl understand how huge America was. Unweariedly he gazed out of the window, and Giacomo persisted in struggling for a place beside him until the other occupants of the compartment, who wanted to play cards, got tired of him and voluntarily surrendered the other window-seat. Karl thanked them—Giacomo's English was not easy for anyone to follow—and in the course of time, as is inevitable among fellow-travellers, they grew much more friendly, although their friendliness was sometimes a nuisance, as for example whenever they ducked down to rescue a card fallen on the floor, they could not resist giving hearty tweaks to Karl's legs or Giacomo's. Whenever that happened Giacomo always shrieked in renewed surprise and drew his legs up; Karl attempted once to give a kick in return, but suffered the rest of the time in silence. Everything that went on in the little compartment, which was thick with cigarette-smoke in spite of the open window, faded into comparative insignificance before the grandeur of the scene outside.

The first day they travelled through a high range of mountains. Masses of blue-black rock rose in sheer wedges to the railway line; even craning one's neck out of the window, one could not see their summits; narrow, gloomy, jagged valleys opened out and one tried to follow with a pointing finger the direction in which they lost themselves; broad mountain streams appeared, rolling in great waves down on to the foothills and drawing with them a thousand foaming wavelets, plunging underneath the bridges over which the train rushed; and they were so near that the breath of coldness rising from them chilled the skin of one's face.

NOTE: *Kafka broke off his work on this novel with unexpected suddenness. It remained unfinished. From what he told me I know that the incomplete chapter about the Nature Theatre of Oklahoma (a chapter the beginning of which particularly delighted Kafka, so that he used to read it aloud with great effect) was intended to be the concluding chapter of the work and should end on a note of reconciliation. In enigmatic language Kafka used to hint smilingly, that within this "almost limitless" theatre his young hero was going to find again a profession, a stand-by, his freedom, even his old home and his parents, as if by some celestial witchery.* MAX BROD

NOTES ON A DREAM

Theodor Herzl

Begun in Paris around Pentecost 1895.

I HAVE BEEN pounding away for some time at a work of tremendous magnitude. I don't know even now if I will be able to carry it through. It bears the aspects of a mighty dream. For days and weeks it has saturated me to the limits of my consciousness; it goes with me everywhere, hovers behind my ordinary talk, peers at me over the shoulders of my funny little journalistic work, overwhelms and intoxicates me.

What will come of it is still too early to say. However, I have had experience enough to tell me that even as a dream it is remarkable and should be written down—if not as a memorial for mankind, then for my own pleasure and meditation in years to come. Or perhaps as something between these two possibilities—that is, as something for literature. If no action comes out of this romancing, a Romance at least will come out of this activity.

Title: The Promised Land.

I am still puzzled how the idea of writing a novel turned into drafting a practical program, although the change occurred in the past few weeks. It took place in the Unconscious.

Perhaps, after all, the idea is in no way practical, and I am only making a joke of myself when I talk of it earnestly to others. And I wander about merely in a romance?

Even then it is worth while writing down what I have thought out these many days and am still thinking out. . . .

Vienna, April 16, 1896.

In these notes* the Jewish State is pictured now as something real, again as the subject for a novel, because I was not sure at the time whether I dared publish it as a serious proposal.

This accounts for the sudden transitions in which the notes abound; all I cared about was to let no idea escape.

* Originally made in the summer of 1895.

Even what is fantastic in these disconnected jottings may one day be of interest to others—and surely to myself. . . .

Paris, June 6, 1895.

I know perfectly well that the first stages in the procedure are as sound as the most remote. But precisely in the first stages (which everyone can see) there must be no mistakes. Otherwise people will take the whole thing for a fantasy.

This is the order in which we proceed:
1) Raising the money (the syndicate).
2) Begin publicity (which will cost nothing, for the anti-Semites will be only too happy, and I shall break down the liberal opposition by threats of competition).
3) Enrolment of land-seekers.
4) More publicity, on the biggest scale. Europe is to scoff, abuse, in short talk about it.
5) Negotiations with Zion.*
6) Contracts for land purchases.

* Apparently the country which is to grant the concession for a state.

7) Issue of land priorities (one billion).

8) Purchase and building of ships.

9) Continuous enlistment of all who apply; recruitment, distribution, training.

10) Begin propaganda for the big subscription.

11) Departure of expedition to take possession of the land, with news service for the entire press.

12) Choosing and demarcating the land, and sites for main cities.

13) Workers from Russia, etc. build embarcation barracks (on Italian or Dutch coast) first for themselves and then for the subsequent contingents.

14) Fare and freight contracts with railroads. We must earn a big profit on transportation.

15) Exchange of old property for new begins.

16) The wheels already in motion must of course be kept turning; new units of the program are successively geared into movement, until the whole machine is at work!

17) Apply to German Kaiser—for privileges!

June 7, 1895.

Must read Daniel Deronda. (Heinrich) Tewels talks about it. I don't know it.

June 7, 1895, in the Palais Royal gardens.
We must build something on the order of the Palais Royal or the Square of St. Mark.

History. Things cannot improve but must get worse—until the massacres. Governments can no longer prevent it, even if they wanted to. Also there is socialism lurking behind.

Circenses as soon as possible.

German theater, international theater, opera, musical comedy, circus, café-concert, Café Champs Elysées.

The High Priests will wear impressive robes; our cuirassiers, yellow trousers and white tunics; the officers, silver breast-plates.

June 8, 1895.
Dig out and transplant the centers. Entire communities, so that the Jews will feel at home and acclimatize themselves.

First stage: The Rothschilds.
Second stage: the midget millionaires.
Third stage: The little people (mass publicity).
If it comes to the third, the first two will rue the day.

We must not only imitate Paris, Florence, etc.;
we must seek out a Jewish style, one that expresses
our sense of deliverance and freedom.

Bright airy halls, borne on columns.

Breathing space between the towns. Each town to
be like a large house planted in its own garden.

The area between the towns to be given over to
nothing but agriculture and woods. Thereby I prevent over-grown cities, and the towns seem more
rapidly settled.

June 9, 1895.

In the morning.

Today I am again as hard as iron. The faintheart-
edness of the people yesterday gives me all the more
reason for action. Christians of their standing would
be cheerful and full of zest for life. Jews are sad.

Against Palestine is its proximity to Russia and
Europe, its small size, as well as its unaccustomed
climate. In its favor, the mighty legend.

S's brother-in-law, after only two weeks' absence,
is homesick for the Vienna coffee-houses. Therefore
I shall transport over there genuine Vienna cafés.

With these small expedients I ensure the desirable illusion of the old environment. Must give attention to these minute needs; they are very important.

The coffin ship! We also take with us our dead.

Much in these notes will seem absurd, exaggerated, crazy. But if I had exercised self-criticism, as I do in my literary work, my ideas would have been stunted. What is monstrous serves the purpose better than what is dwarfed, for anyone can do the pruning easily enough.

Artists will understand why I have allowed extravagances and dreams to run riot among my practical, political, and legislative ideas—as grass sprouts up between the stones of a pavement. I could not permit myself to be tied down purely to sober fact. Intoxication was necessary.

Yes, artists will understand this. But there are so few artists.

Perhaps I shall make a distinction, in the book, between the two dream worlds which mingle in a common flow, by printing the fantasy in a different type. Thus the lover of such things will see at once where and in what way the grass grows—others will hear it grow—and the rest will recognize the solid paving stones.

June 12, 1895.

To the architects:

Typical designs of workshops for shoemakers, tailors, carpenters, etc.—designs to be reproduced and distributed abroad in countless number.

This is an advertisement to attract immigrants!

Work will be a joy. Everyone, if possible, to attain a little house of his own. . . .

Am I working it out? No, it is working itself out through me.

It would be an obsession if it were not so rational from beginning to end.

This is what used to be called "inspiration."

When I say God I do not mean to offend the free-thinkers. For my part they can say World Spirit or any other term in place of this beloved old wonderful abbreviation by which I touch the simplest understanding. For in our theological battle-of-words we ultimately mean the same thing. In belief or in doubt we mean the same thing: that it is inexplicable.

June 14, 1895.

This morning, a severe headache. In order to divert the blood from my head, I will begin today to learn bicycling. Otherwise I won't be able to carry through the task.

June 16, 1895.

No one has ever thought of looking for the Promised Land in the place where it really is—and yet it lies so near.

It is here: within ourselves!

I am not misleading anyone. Everyone can satisfy himself that I am telling the truth. For everyone will carry over there, in himself, a piece of the Promised Land. This one, in his head, that one, in his hands; the third, in his savings. The Promised Land is where we carry it.

I believe that for me life has ended and world history has begun.

June 16, 1895.

S was with me today and chaffed me, saying that I looked as though I had invented the dirigible airship.

H'm, perhaps! I thought to myself, and was silent.

June 17, 1895.

S says: it is a thing someone tried to accomplish in the last century. . . .

Yes, in the last century it was impossible. But now it is possible, for we have machines.

June 22, 1895.

At bottom I am like the dish-washer who has drawn the grand prize in the lottery, and an hour later says with a shrug: "Pooh, what are a hundred thousand florins?" . . .

As of now, I believe that putting my plan into action will find and leave me tranquil. Not so long ago, the thought of it filled me with anxiety. If, that is, I should convince Bismarck.

If I do not, or if he even declines to see me—well, the whole thing was a romance. Oh, an immortal romance!

That too is something.

THE BOOK
OF THE MACHINE

Samuel Butler

IT WAS during my stay in City of the Colleges of Unreason—a city whose Erewhonian name is so cacophonous that I refrain from giving it—that I learned the particulars of the revolution which had ended in the destruction of so many of the mechanical inventions which were formerly in common use.

Mr. Thims took me to the rooms of a gentleman who had a great reputation for learning, but who was also, so Mr. Thims told me, rather a dangerous person, inasmuch as he had attempted to introduce an adverb into the hypothetical language. He had heard of my watch and been exceedingly anxious to see me, for he was accounted the most learned antiquary in Erewhon on the subject of mechanical lore.

We fell to talking upon the subject, and when I left he gave me a reprinted copy of the work which brought the revolution about.

It had taken place some five hundred years before my arrival: people had long become thoroughly used to the change, although at the time that it was made the country was plunged into the deepest misery, and a reaction which followed had very nearly proved successful. Civil war raged for many years, and is said to have reduced the number of inhabitants by one-half. The parties were styled the machinists and the anti-machinists, and in the end, as I have said already, the latter got the victory, treating their opponents with such unparalleled severity that they extirpated every trace of opposition.

The wonder was that they allowed any mechanical appliances to remain in the kingdom, neither do I believe that they would have done so, had not the Professors of Inconsistency and Evasion made a stand against the carrying of the new principles to their legitimate conclusions. These Professors, moreover, insisted that during the struggle the anti-machinists should use every known improvement in the art of war, and several new weapons, offensive and defensive, were invented, while it was in progress. I was surprised at there remaining so many mechanical specimens as are seen in the museums, and at students having rediscovered their past uses so completely; for at the time of the revolution the victors wrecked all the more complicated machines, and burned all treatises on mechanics, and all engineers' workshops—thus, so they thought, cutting the mischief out root and branch, at an incalculable cost of blood and treasure.

Certainly they had not spared their labor, but work of this description can never be perfectly achieved, and when, some two hundred years before my arrival, all passion upon the subject had cooled down, and no one save a lunatic would have dreamed of reintroducing forbidden inventions, the subject came to be regarded as a curious antiquarian study, like that of some long-forgotten religious practices among ourselves. Then came the careful search for whatever fragments could be found, and for any machines that might have been hidden away, and also numberless treatises were written, showing what the functions of each rediscovered machine had been; all being done with no idea of using such machinery again, but with the feelings of an English antiquarian concerning Druidical monuments or flint arrow heads.

On my return to the metropolis, during the remaining weeks or rather days of my sojourn in Erewhon I made a *résumé* in English of the work which brought about the already mentioned revolution. My ignorance of technical terms has led me doubtless into many errors, and I have occasionally, where I found translation impossible, substituted purely English names and ideas for the original Erewhonian ones, but the reader may rely on my general accuracy. I have thought it best to insert my translation here.

THE BOOK OF THE MACHINES
(Excerpts)

"There is no security against the ultimate development of mechanical consciousness, in the fact of machines possessing little consciousness now. A mollusc has not much consciousness. Reflect upon the extraordinary advance which machines have made during the last few hundred years, and note how slowly the animal and vegetable kingdoms are advancing. The more highly organized machines are creatures not so much of yesterday, as of the last five minutes, so to speak, in comparison with past time. Assume for the sake of argument that conscious beings have existed for some twenty million years: see what strides machines have made in the last thousand! May not the world last twenty million years longer? If so, what will they not in the end become? Is it not safer to nip the mischief in the bud and to forbid them further progress?

"Do not let me be misunderstood as living in fear of any actually existing machine; there is probably no known machine which is more than a prototype of future mechanical life. The present machines are to the future as the early Saurians to man. The largest of them will probably greatly diminish in size. Some of the lowest vertebrata attained a much greater bulk than has descended to their more highly organized living representatives, and in like manner a diminution in the size of machines has often attended their development and progress.

"Take the watch, for example; examine its beautiful structure; observe the intelligent play of the minute members which compose it: yet this little creature is but a development of the cumbrous clocks that preceded it; it is no deterioration from them. A day may come when clocks, which certainly at the present time are not diminishing in bulk, will be superseded owing to the universal use of watches, in which case they will become as extinct as ichthyosauri, while the watch, whose tendency has for some years been to decrease in size rather than the contrary, will remain the only existing type of an extinct race.

"But returning to the argument, I would repeat that I fear none of the existing machines; what I fear is the extraordinary rapidity with which they are becoming something very different to what they are at present. No class of beings have in any time past made so rapid a movement forward. Should not that movement be jealously watched, and checked while we can still check it? And is it not necessary for this end to destroy the more advanced of the machines which are in use at present, though it is admitted that they are in themselves harmless?

"It is possible that by that time children will learn the differential calculus—as they learn now to speak —from their mothers and nurses, or that they may talk in the hypothetical language, and work rule of three sums, as soon as they are born; but this is not probable; we cannot calculate on any corresponding advance in man's intellectual or physical powers which shall be a set-off against the far greater development which seems in store for the machines. Some people may say that man's moral influence will suffice to rule them; but I cannot think it will ever be safe to repose much trust in the moral sense of any machine.

"And take man's vaunted power of calculation. Have we not engines which can do all manner of sums more quickly and correctly than we can? What prizeman in Hypothetics at any of our Colleges of Unreason can compare with some of these machines in their own line? In fact, wherever precision is required man flies to the machine at once, as far preferable to himself. Our sum-engines never drop a figure, nor our looms a stitch; the machine is brisk and active, when the man is weary; it is clear-headed and collected, when the man is stupid and dull; it needs no slumber, when man must sleep or drop; ever at its post, ever ready for work, its alacrity never flags, its patience never gives in; its might is stronger than combined hundreds, and swifter than the flight of birds; it can burrow beneath the earth, and walk upon the largest rivers and sink not. This is the green tree; what then shall be done in the dry?

"Who shall say that a man does see or hear? He is such a hive and swarm of parasites that it is doubtful whether his body is not more theirs than his, and whether he is anything but another kind of ant-heap after all. May not man himself become a sort of parasite upon the machines? An affectionate machine-tickling aphid?

"True, from a low materialistic point of view, it would seem that those thrive best who use machinery wherever its use is possible with profit; but this is the art of the machines—they serve that they may rule. They bear no malice towards man for destroying a whole race of them provided he creates a better instead; on the contrary, they reward him liberally for having hastened their development. It is for neglecting them that he incurs their wrath, or for using inferior machines, or for not making sufficient exertions to invent new ones, or for destroying them without replacing them; yet these are the very things we ought to do, and do quickly; for though our rebellion against their infant power will cause infinite suffering, what will not things come to, if that rebellion is delayed?

"They have preyed upon man's groveling preference for his material over his spiritual interests, and have betrayed him into supplying that element of struggle and warfare without which no race can advance. The lower animals progress because they struggle with one another; the weaker die, the stronger breed and transmit their strength. The machines being of themselves unable to struggle, have got man to do their struggling for them: as long as he fulfills this function duly, all goes well with him —at least he thinks so; but the moment he fails to do his best for the advancement of machinery by encouraging the good and destroying the bad, he is left behind in the race of competition; and this means that he will be made uncomfortable in a variety of ways, and perhaps die.

"So that even now the machines will only serve on condition of being served, and that too upon their own terms; the moment their terms are not complied with, they jib, and either smash both themselves and all whom they can reach, or turn churlish and refuse to work at all. How many men at this hour are living in a state of bondage to the machines? How many spend their whole lives, from the cradle to the grave, in tending them by night and day? Is it not plain that the machines are gaining ground upon us, when we reflect on the increasing number of those who are bound down to them as slaves, and of those who devote their whole souls to the advancement of the mechanical kingdom?

"Herein lies our danger. For many seem inclined to acquiesce in so dishonorable a future. They say that although man should become to the machines what the horse and dog are to us, yet that he will continue to exist, and will probably be better off in a state of domestication under the beneficent rule of the machines than in his present wild condition. We treat our domestic animals with much kindness. We give them whatever we believe to be the best for them; and there can be no doubt that our use of meat has increased their happiness rather than detracted from it. In like manner there is reason to hope that the machines will use us kindly, for their existence will be in a great measure dependent upon ours; they will rule us with a rod of iron, but they will not eat us; they will not only require our services in the reproduction and education of their young, but also in waiting upon them as servants; in gathering food for them, and feeding them; in restoring them to health when they are sick; and in either burying their dead or working up their deceased members into new forms of mechanical existence.

"The very nature of the motive power which works the advancement of the machines precludes the possibility of man's life being rendered miserable as well as enslaved. Slaves are tolerably happy if they have good masters, and the revolution will not occur in our time, nor hardly in ten thousand years, or ten times that. Is it wise to be uneasy about a contingency which is so remote? Man is not a sentimental animal where his material interests are concerned, and though here and there some ardent soul may look upon himself and curse his fate that he was not born a vapor-engine, yet the mass of mankind will acquiesce in any arrangement which gives them better food and clothing at a cheaper rate, and will refrain from yielding to unreasonable jealousy merely because there are other destinies more glorious than their own.

"The power of custom is enormous, and so gradual will be the change, that man's sense of what is due to himself will be at no time rudely shocked; our bondage will steal upon us noiselessly and by imperceptible approaches; nor will there ever be such a clashing of desires between man and the machines as will lead to an encounter between them. Among themselves the machines will war eternally, but they will still require man as the being through whose agency the struggle will be principally conducted. In point of fact there is no occasion for anxiety about the future happiness of man so long as he continues to be in any way profitable to the machines; he may become the inferior race, but he will be infinitely better off than he is now. Is it not then both absurd and unreasonable to be envious of our benefactors? And should we not be guilty of consummate folly if we were to reject the advantages which we cannot obtain otherwise, merely because they involve a greater gain to others than to ourselves?

"With those who can argue in this way I have nothing in common. I shrink with as much horror from believing that my race can ever be superseded or surpassed, as I should do from believing that even at the remotest period my ancestors were other than human beings. Could I believe that ten hundred thousand years ago a single one of my ancestors was another kind of being to myself, I should lose all self-respect, and take no further pleasure or interest in life. I have the same feeling with regard to my descendants, and believe it to be one that will be felt so generally that the country will resolve upon putting an immediate stop to all further mechanical progress, and upon destroying all improvements that have been made for the last three hundred years. I would not urge more than this. We may trust ourselves to deal with those that remain, and though I should prefer to have seen the destruction include another two hundred years, I am aware of the necessity for compromising, and would so far sacrifice my own individual convictions as to be content with three hundred. Less than this will be insufficient."

This was the conclusion of the attack which led to the destruction of machinery throughout Erewhon ... and in the end succeeded in destroying all the inventions that had been discovered for the preceding 271 years, a period which was agreed upon by all parties after several years of wrangling as to whether a certain kind of mangle which was much in use among washerwomen should be saved or no. It was at last ruled to be dangerous, and was just excluded by the limit of 271 years. Then came the reactionary civil wars which nearly ruined the country, but which it would be beyond my present scope to describe.

PARADISE (TO BE) REGAINED

Henry David Thoreau

A review of the book
The Paradise within the Reach of All Men,
without Labor, by Powers of Nature and
Machinery. An Address to All Intelligent Men.
By J. A. Etzler. London, 1842.

W E LEARN that Mr. Etzler is a native of Germany, and originally published his book in Pennsylvania, ten or twelve years ago; and now a second English edition, from the original American one, is demanded by his readers across the water, owing, we suppose, to the recent spread of Fourier's doctrines. It is one of the signs of the times. We confess that we have risen from reading this book with enlarged ideas, and grander conceptions of our duties in this world. It did expand us a little. It is worth attending to, if only that it entertains large questions. Consider what Mr. Etzler proposes:

"Fellow-men! I promise to show the means of creating a paradise within ten years, where everything desirable for human life may be had by every man in superabundance, without labor, and without pay; where the whole face of nature shall be changed into the most beautiful forms, and man may live in the most magnificent palaces, in all imaginable refinements of luxury, and in the most delightful gardens; where he may accomplish, without labor, in one year, more than hitherto could be done in thousands of years; may level mountains, sink valleys, create lakes, drain lakes and swamps, and intersect the land everywhere with beautiful canals, and roads for transporting heavy loads of many thousand tons, and for travelling one thousand miles in twenty-four hours; may cover the ocean with floating islands movable in any desired direction with immense power and celerity, in perfect security, and with all comforts and luxuries, bearing gardens and palaces, with thousands of families, and provided with rivulets of sweet water; may explore the interior of the globe, and travel from pole to pole in a fortnight; provide himself with means, unheard of yet, for increasing his knowledge of the world, and so his intelligence; lead a life of continual happiness, of enjoyments yet unknown; free himself from almost all the evils that afflict mankind, except death, and even put death far beyond the common period of human life, and finally render it less afflicting. Mankind may thus live in and enjoy a new world, far superior to the present, and raise themselves far higher in the scale of being."

It would seem from this and various indications beside, that there is a transcendentalism in mechanics as well as in ethics. While the whole field of the one reformer lies beyond the boundaries of space, the other is pushing his schemes for the elevation of the race to its utmost limits. While one scours the heavens, the other sweeps the earth. One says he will reform himself, and then nature and circumstances will be right. Let us not obstruct ourselves, for that is the greatest friction. It is of little importance though a cloud obstruct the view of the astronomer compared with his own blindness. The other will reform nature and circumstances, and then man will be right. . . .

Let us not succumb to nature. We will marshal the clouds and restrain tempests; we will bottle up pestilent exhalations; we will probe for earthquakes, grub them up, and give vent to the dangerous gas; we will disembowel the volcano, and extract its poison, take its seed out. We will wash water, and warm fire, and cool ice, and underprop the earth. We will teach birds to fly, and fishes to swim, and ruminants to chew the cud. It is time we had looked into these things.

And it becomes the moralist, too, to inquire what man might do to improve and beautify the system; what to make the stars shine more brightly, the sun more cheery and joyous, the moon more placid and content. Could he not heighten the tints of flowers and the melody of birds? Does he perform his duty to the inferior races? Should he not be a god to them? What is the part of magnanimity to the whale and the beaver? Should we not fear to exchange places with them for a day, lest by their behavior they should shame us? Might we not treat with magnanimity the shark and the tiger, not descend to meet them on their own level, with spears of shark's teeth and bucklers of tiger's skin? We slander the hyena; man is the fiercest and cruelest animal. Ah! he is of little faith; even the erring comets and meteors would thank him, and return his kindness in their kind.

How meanly and grossly do we deal with nature! Could we not have a less gross labor? What else do these fine inventions suggest—magnetism, the daguerreotype, electricity? Can we not do more than cut and trim the forest?—can we not assist in its interior economy, in the circulation of the sap? Now we work superficially and violently. We do not suspect how much might be done to improve our relation to animated nature even; what kindness and refined courtesy there might be.

It is a rather serious objection to Mr. Etzler's schemes, that they require time, men, and money, three very superfluous and inconvenient things for an honest and well-disposed man to deal with. "The whole world," he tells us, "might therefore be really changed into a paradise, within less than ten years, commencing from the first year of an association for the purpose of constructing and applying the machinery." We are sensible of a startling incongruity when time and money are mentioned in this connection. The ten years which are proposed would be a tedious while to wait, if every man were at his post and did his duty, but quite too short a period, if we are to take time for it. But this fault is by no means peculiar to Mr. Etzler's schemes. There is far too much hurry and bustle, and too little patience and privacy, in all our methods, as if something were to be accomplished in centuries. The true reformer does not want time, nor money, nor coöperation, nor advice. What is time but the stuff delay is made of? And depend upon it, our virtue will not live on the interest of our money. He expects no income, but outgoes; so soon as we begin to count the cost, the cost begins. And as for advice, the information floating in the atmosphere of society is as evanescent and unserviceable to him as gossamer for clubs of Hercules. There is absolutely no common sense; it is common nonsense. If we are to risk a cent or a drop of our blood, who then shall advise us? For ourselves, we are too young for experience. Who is old enough? We are older by faith than by experience. In the unbending of the arm to do the deed there is experience worth all the maxims in the world.

"It will now be plainly seen that the execution of the proposals is not proper for individuals. Whether it be proper for government at this time, before the subject has become popular, is a question to be decided; all that is to be done is to step forth, after mature reflection, to confess loudly one's conviction, and to constitute societies. Man is powerful but in union with many. Nothing great, for the improvement of his own condition, or that of his fellow-men, can ever be effected by individual enterprise."

Alas! this is the crying sin of the age, this want of faith in the prevalence of a man. Nothing can be effected but by one man. He who wants help wants everything. True, this is the condition of our weakness, but it can never be the means of our recovery. We must first succeed alone, that we may enjoy our success together. We trust that the social movements which we witness indicate an aspiration not to be thus cheaply satisfied. In this matter of reforming the world, we have little faith in corporations; not thus was it first formed. . . .

Faith, indeed, is all the reform that is needed; it is itself a reform. Doubtless, we are as slow to conceive of Paradise as of Heaven, of a perfect natural as of a perfect spiritual world. We see how past ages have loitered and erred. "Is perhaps our generation free from irrationality and error? Have we perhaps reached now the summit of human wisdom, and need no more to look out for mental or physical improvement?" Undoubtedly, we are never so visionary as to be prepared for what the next hour may bring forth.

Μέλλει τὸ θεῖον δ᾽ ἐστι τοιοῦτον φύσει.

The Divine is about to be, and such is its nature. In our wisest moments we are secreting a matter, which, like the lime of the shellfish, incrusts us quite over, and well for us if, like it, we cast our shells from time to time, though they be pearl and of fairest tint. Let us consider under what disadvantages Science has hitherto labored before we pronounce thus confidently on her progress.

Mr. Etzler is not one of the enlightened practical men, the pioneers of the actual, who move with the slow, deliberate tread of science, conserving the world; who execute the dreams of the last century, though they have no dreams of their own; yet he deals in the very raw but still solid material of all inventions. He has more of the practical than usually belongs to so bold a schemer, so resolute a dreamer. Yet his success is in theory, and not in practice, and he feeds our faith rather than contents our understanding. His book wants order, serenity, dignity, everything—but it does not fail to impart what only man can impart to man of much importance, his own faith. It is true his dreams are not thrilling nor bright enough, and he leaves off to dream where he who dreams just before the dawn begins. His castles in the air fall to the ground, because they are not built lofty enough; they should be secured to heaven's roof. After all, the theories and speculations of men concern us more than their puny accomplishment. It is with a certain coldness and languor that we loiter about the actual and so-called practical. How little do the most wonderful inventions of modern times detain us. They insult nature. Every machine, or particular application, seems a slight outrage against universal laws. How many fine inventions are there which do not clutter the ground? We think that those only succeed which minister to our sensible and animal wants, which bake or brew, wash or warm, or the like. But are those of no account which are patented by fancy and imagination, and succeed so admirably in our dreams that they give the tone still to our waking thoughts? Already nature is serving all those uses which science slowly derives on a much higher and grander scale to him that will be served by her. When the sunshine falls on the path of the poet, he enjoys all those pure benefits and pleasures which the arts slowly and partially realize from age to age. The winds which fan his cheek waft him the sum of that profit and happiness which their lagging inventions supply.

The chief fault of this book is, that it aims to secure the greatest degree of gross comfort and pleasure merely. It paints a Mahometan's heaven, and stops short with singular abruptness when we think it is drawing near to the precincts of the Christian's —and we trust we have not made here a distinction without a difference. Undoubtedly if we were to reform this outward life truly and thoroughly, we should find no duty of the inner omitted. It would be employment for our whole nature; and what we should do thereafter would be as vain a question as to ask the bird what it will do when its nest is built and its brood reared. But a moral reform must take place first, and then the necessity of the other will be superseded, and we shall sail and plow by its force alone. There is a speedier way than the "Mechanical System" can show to fill up marshes, to drown the roar of the waves, to tame hyenas, secure agreeable environs, diversify the land, and refresh it with "rivulets of sweet water," and that is by the power of rectitude and true behavior. It is only for a little while, only occasionally, methinks, that we want a garden. Surely a good man need not be at the labor to level a hill for the sake of a prospect, or raise fruits and flowers, and construct floating islands, for the sake of a paradise. He enjoys better prospects than lie behind any hill. Where an angel travels it will be paradise all the way, but where Satan travels it will be burning marl and cinders. What says Veeshnoo Sarma? "He whose mind is at ease is possessed of all riches. Is it not the same to one whose foot is inclosed in a shoe, as if the whole surface of the earth were covered with leather?"

He who is conversant with the supernal powers will not worship these inferior deities of the wind, waves, tide, and sunshine. But we would not disparage the importance of such calculations as we have described. They are truths in physics, because they are true in ethics. The moral powers no one would presume to calculate. Suppose we could compare the moral with the physical, and say how many horse-power the force of love, for instance, blowing on every square foot of a man's soul, would equal. No doubt we are well aware of this force; figures would not increase our respect for it; the sunshine is equal to but one ray of its heat. The light of the sun is but the shadow of love. "The souls of men loving and fearing God," says Raleigh, "receive influence from that divine light itself, whereof the sun's clarity, and that of the stars, is by Plato called but a shadow. *Lumen est umbra Dei, Deus est Lumen Luminis.* Light is the shadow of God's brightness, who is the light of light," and, we may add, the heat of heat. Love is the wind, the tide, the waves, the sunshine. Its power is incalculable; it is many horse-power. It never ceases, it never slacks; it can move the globe without a resting-place; it can warm without fire; it can feed without meat; it can clothe without garments; it can shelter without roof; it can make a paradise within which will dispense with a paradise without. But though the wisest men in all ages have labored to publish this force, and every human heart is, sooner or later, more or less, made to feel it, yet how little is actually applied to social ends! True, it is the motive-power of all successful social machinery; but as in physics we have made the elements do only a little drudgery for us—steam to take the place of a few horses, wind of a few oars, water of a few cranks and handmills—as the mechanical forces have not yet been generously and largely applied to make the physical world answer to the ideal, so the power of love has been but meanly and sparingly applied, as yet. It has patented only such machines as the almshouse, the hospital, and the Bible Society, while its infinite wind is still blowing, and blowing down these very structures too, from time to time. Still less are we accumulating its power, and preparing to act with greater energy at a future time. Shall we not contribute our shares to this enterprise, then?

THE TAILOR OF GLOUCESTER

Beatrix Potter

IN the time of swords and periwigs and full-skirted coats with flowered lappets—when gentlemen wore ruffles, and gold-laced waistcoats of paduasoy and taffeta—there lived a tailor in Gloucester.

He sat in the window of a little shop in Westgate Street, cross-legged on a table, from morning till dark.

All day long while the light lasted he sewed and snippeted, piecing out his satin and pompadour, and lutestring; stuffs had strange names, and were very expensive in the days of the Tailor of Gloucester.

But although he sewed fine silk for his neighbours, he himself was very, very poor—a little old man in spectacles, with a pinched face, old crooked fingers, and a suit of thread-bare clothes.

He cut his coats without waste, according to his

embroidered cloth; they were very small ends and snippets that lay about upon the table—"Too narrow breadths for nought—except waistcoats for mice," said the tailor.

One bitter cold day near Christmastime the tailor began to make a coat—a coat of cherry-coloured corded silk embroidered with pansies and roses, and a cream coloured satin waistcoat—trimmed with gauze and green worsted chenille—for the Mayor of Gloucester.

The tailor worked and worked, and he talked to himself. He measured the silk, and turned it round and round, and trimmed it into shape with his shears; the table was all littered with cherry-coloured snippets.

"No breadth at all, and cut on the cross; it is no breadth at all; tippets for mice and ribbons for mobs! for mice!" said the Tailor of Gloucester.

When the snow-flakes came down against the small leaded window-panes and shut out the light, the tailor had done his day's work; all the silk and satin lay cut out upon the table.

There were twelve pieces for the coat and four pieces for the waistcoat; and there were pocket flaps and cuffs, and buttons all in order. For the lining of the coat there was fine yellow taffeta; and for the button-holes of the waistcoat, there was cherry-coloured twist. And everything was ready to sew together in the morning, all measured and sufficient —except that there was wanting just one single skein of cherry-coloured twisted silk.

The tailor came out of his shop at dark, for he did not sleep there at nights; he fastened the window and locked the door, and took away the key. No one lived there at night but little brown mice, and they run in and out without any keys!

For behind the wooden wainscots of all the old houses in Gloucester, there are little mouse stair-cases and secret trap-doors; and the mice run from house to house through those long narrow passages; they can run all over the town without going into the streets.

But the tailor came out of his shop, and shuffled home through the snow. He lived quite near by in College Court, next the doorway to College Green; and although it was not a big house, the tailor was so poor he only rented the kitchen.

He lived alone with his cat; it was called Simpkin.

Now all day long while the tailor was out at work, Simpkin kept house by himself; and he also was fond of the mice, though he gave them no satin for coats!

"Miaw?" said the cat when the tailor opened the door. "Miaw?"

The tailor replied—"Simpkin, we shall make our fortune, but I am worn to a ravelling. Take this groat (which is our last fourpence) and Simpkin, take a china pipkin; buy a penn'orth of bread, a penn'orth of milk and a penn'orth of sausages. And oh, Simpkin, with the last penny of our fourpence buy me one penn'orth of cherry-coloured silk. But do not lose the last penny of the fourpence, Simpkin, or I am undone and worn to a threadpaper, for I have NO MORE TWIST."

Then Simpkin again said, "Miaw?" and took the groat and the pipkin, and went out into the dark.

The tailor was very tired and beginning to be ill. He sat down by the hearth and talked to himself about that wonderful coat.

"I shall make my fortune—to be cut bias—the Mayor of Gloucester is to be married on Christmas Day in the morning, and he hath ordered a coat and an embroidered waistcoat—to be lined with yellow taffeta—and the taffeta sufficeth; there is no more left over in snippets than will serve to make tippets for mice——"

Then the tailor started; for suddenly, interrupting him, from the dresser at the other side of the kitchen came a number of little noises—

Tip tap, tip tap, tip tap tip!

"Now what can that be?" said the Tailor of Gloucester, jumping up from his chair. The dresser was covered with crockery and pipkins, willow pattern plates, and tea-cups and mugs.

The tailor crossed the kitchen, and stood quite still beside the dresser, listening, and peering through his spectacles. Again from under a tea-cup, came those funny little noises—

Tip tap, tip tap, tip tap tip!

"This is very peculiar," said the Tailor of Gloucester; and he lifted up the tea-cup which was upside down.

Out stepped a little live lady mouse, and made a curtsey to the tailor! Then she hopped away down off the dresser, and under the wainscot.

The tailor sat down again by the fire, warming

his poor cold hands, and mumbling to himself——

"The waistcoat is cut out from peach-coloured satin—tambour stitch and rose-buds in beautiful floss silk. Was I wise to entrust my last fourpence to Simpkin? One-and-twenty button-holes of cherry-coloured twist!"

But all at once, from the dresser, there came other little noises:

Tip tap, tip tap, tip tap tip!

"This is passing extraordinary!" said the Tailor of Gloucester, and turned over another tea-cup, which was upside down.

Out stepped a little gentleman mouse, and made a bow to the tailor!

And then from all over the dresser came a chorus of little tappings, all sounding together, and answering one another, like watch-beetles in an old worm-eaten window-shutter—

Tip tap, tip tap, tip tap tip!

And out from under tea-cups and from under bowls and basins, stepped other and more little mice who hopped away down off the dresser and under the wainscot.

The tailor sat down, close over the fire, lamenting—"One-and-twenty button-holes of cherry-coloured silk! To be finished by noon of Saturday: and this is Tuesday evening. Was it right to let loose those mice, undoubtedly the property of Simpkin? Alack, I am undone, for I have no more twist!"

The little mice came out again, and listened to the tailor; they took notice of the pattern of that wonderful coat. They whispered to one another about the taffeta lining, and about little mouse tippets.

And then all at once they all ran away together down the passage behind the wainscot, squeaking and calling to one another, as they ran from house to house; and not one mouse was left in the tailor's kitchen when Simpkin came back with the pipkin of milk!

Simpkin opened the door and bounced in, with an angry "G-r-r-miaw!" like a cat that is vexed: for he hated the snow, and there was snow in his ears, and snow in his collar at the back of his neck. He put down the loaf and the sausages upon the dresser, and sniffed.

"Simpkin," said the tailor, "where is my twist?"

But Simpkin set down the pipkin of milk upon the dresser, and looked suspiciously at the tea-cups. He wanted his supper of little fat mouse!

"Simpkin," said the tailor, "where is my TWIST?"

But Simpkin hid a little parcel privately in the tea-pot, and spit and growled at the tailor; and if Simpkin had been able to talk, he would have asked: "Where is my MOUSE?"

"Alack, I am undone!" said the Tailor of Gloucester, and went sadly to bed.

All that night long Simpkin hunted and searched through the kitchen, peeping into cupboards and under the wainscot, and into the tea-pot where he had hidden that twist; but still he found never a mouse!

Whenever the tailor muttered and talked in his sleep, Simpkin said "Miaw-ger-r-w-s-s-ch!" and made strange horrid noises, as cats do at night.

For the poor old tailor was very ill with a fever, tossing and turning in his four-post bed; and still in his dreams he mumbled—"No more twist! no more twist!"

All that day he was ill, and the next day, and the next; and what should become of the cherry-coloured coat? In the tailor's shop in Westgate Street the embroidered silk and satin lay cut out upon the table—one-and-twenty button-holes—and who should come to sew them, when the window was barred, and the door was fast locked?

But that does not hinder the little brown mice; they run in and out without any keys through all the old houses in Gloucester!

Out of doors the market folks went trudging through the snow to buy their geese and turkeys, and to bake their Christmas pies; but there would be no Christmas dinner for Simpkin and the poor old Tailor of Gloucester.

The tailor lay ill for three days and nights; and then it was Christmas Eve, and very late at night. The moon climbed up over the roofs and chimneys, and looked down over the gateway into College Court. There were no lights in the windows, nor any sound in the houses; all the city of Gloucester was fast asleep under the snow.

And still Simpkin wanted his mice, and he mewed as he stood beside the four-post bed.

But it is in the old story that all the beasts can talk, in the night between Christmas Eve and Christmas Day in the morning (though there are very few folk that can hear them, or know what it is that they say).

When the Cathedral clock struck twelve there was an answer—like an echo of the chimes—and Simpkin heard it, and came out of the tailor's door, and wandered about in the snow.

From all the roofs and gables and old wooden houses in Gloucester came a thousand merry voices singing the old Christmas rhymes—all the old songs that ever I heard of, and some that I don't know, like Whittington's bells.

First and loudest the cocks cried out: "Dame, get up, and bake your pies!"

"Oh, dilly, dilly, dilly!" sighed Simpkin.

And now in a garret there were lights and sounds of dancing, and cats came from over the way.

"Hey, diddle, diddle, the cat and the fiddle! All the cats in Gloucester—except me," said Simpkin.

Under the wooden eaves the starlings and sparrows sang of Christmas pies; the jack-daws woke up in the Cathedral tower; and although it was the middle of the night the throstles and robins sang; the air was quite full of little twittering tunes.

But it was all rather provoking to poor hungry Simpkin!

Particularly he was vexed with some little shrill

voices from behind a wooden lattice. I think that they were bats, because they always have very small voices—especially in a black frost, when they talk in their sleep, like the Tailor of Gloucester.

They said something mysterious that sounded like—

"Buz, quoth the blue fly; hum, quoth the bee;
Buz and hum they cry, and so do we!"

and Simpkin went away shaking his ears as if he had a bee in his bonnet.

From the tailor's shop in Westgate came a glow of light; and when Simpkin crept up to peep in at the window it was full of candles. There was a snippeting of scissors, and snappeting of thread; and little mouse voices sang loudly and gaily—

"Four-and-twenty tailors
Went to catch a snail,
The best man amongst them
Durst not touch her tail;
She put out her horns
Like a little kyloe cow,
Run, tailors, run! or she'll have you all e'en now!"

Then without a pause the little mouse voices went on again—

"Sieve my lady's oatmeal,
Grind my lady's flour,
Put it in a chestnut,
Let it stand an hour——"

"Mew! Mew!" interrupted Simpkin, and he scratched at the door. But the key was under the tailor's pillow, he could not get in.

The little mice only laughed, and tried another tune—

"Three little mice sat down to spin,
Pussy passed by and she peeped in.
What are you at, my fine little men?
Making coats for gentlemen.
Shall I come in and cut off your threads?
Oh, no, Miss Pussy, you'd bite off our heads!"

"Mew! Mew!" cried Simpkin. "Hey diddle dinketty?" answered the little mice—

"Hey diddle dinketty, poppetty pet!
The merchants of London they wear scarlet;
Silk in the collar, and gold in the hem,
So merrily march the merchantmen!"

They clicked their thimbles to mark the time, but none of the songs pleased Simpkin; he sniffed and mewed at the door of the shop.

"And then I bought
A pipkin and a popkin,
A slipkin and a slopkin,
All for one farthing——

and upon the kitchen dresser!" added the rude little mice.

"Mew! scratch! scratch!" scuffled Simpkin on the window-sill; while the little mice inside sprang to their feet, and all began to shout at once in little twittering voices: "No more twist! No more twist!" And they barred up the window shutters and shut out Simpkin.

But still through the nicks in the shutters he could hear the click of thimbles, and little mouse voices singing—

"No more twist! No more twist!"

Simpkin came away from the shop and went home, considering in his mind. He found the poor old tailor without fever, sleeping peacefully.

Then Simpkin went on tip-toe and took a little parcel of silk out of the tea-pot, and looked at it in the moonlight; and he felt quite ashamed of his badness compared with those good little mice!

When the tailor awoke in the morning, the first

thing which he saw upon the patchwork quilt was a skein of cherry-coloured twisted silk, and beside his bed stood the repentant Simpkin!

"Alack, I am worn to a ravelling," said the Tailor of Gloucester, "but I have my twist!"

The sun was shining on the snow when the tailor got up and dressed, and came out into the street with Simpkin running before him.

The starlings whistled on the chimney stacks, and the throstles and robins sang—but they sang their own little noises, not the words they had sung in the night.

"Alack," said the tailor, "I have my twist; but no more strength—nor time—than will serve to make me one single button-hole; for this is Christmas Day in the Morning! The Mayor of Gloucester shall be married by noon—and where is his cherry-coloured coat?"

He unlocked the door of the little shop in West-gate Street, and Simpkin ran in, like a cat that expects something.

But there was no one there! Not even one little brown mouse!

The boards were swept clean; the little ends of

thread and the little silk snippets were all tidied away, and gone from off the floor.

But upon the table—oh joy! the tailor gave a shout—there, where he had left plain cuttings of silk—there lay the most beautifullest coat and embroidered satin waistcoat that ever were worn by a Mayor of Gloucester.

There were roses and pansies upon the facings of the coat; and the waistcoat was worked with poppies and corn-flowers.

Everything was finished except just one single cherry-coloured button-hole, and where that button-hole was wanting there was pinned a scrap of paper with these words—in little teeny weeny writing—

NO MORE TWIST

And from then began the luck of the Tailor of Gloucester; he grew quite stout, and he grew quite rich.

He made the most wonderful waistcoats for all the rich merchants of Gloucester, and for all the fine gentlemen of the country round.

Never were seen such ruffles, or such embroidered

cuffs and lappets! But his button-holes were the greatest triumph of it all.

The stitches of those button-holes were so neat—*so* neat—I wonder how they could be stitched by an old man in spectacles, with crooked old fingers, and a tailor's thimble.

The stitches of those button-holes were so small—*so* small—they looked as if they had been made by little mice!

OUT OF THE FOUNTAIN

Doris Lessing

I COULD BEGIN, There was once a man called Ephraim who lived in . . . but for me this story begins with a fog. Fog in Paris delayed a flight to London by a couple of hours, and so a group of travellers sat around a table drinking coffee and entertaining each other.

A woman from Texas joked that a week before she had thrown coins into the fountain in Rome for luck—and had been dogged by minor ill fortune ever since. A Canadian said he had spent far too much money on a holiday and at the same fountain three days ago had been tempted to lift coins out with a magnet when no one was looking. Someone said that in a Berlin theatre last night there had been a scene where a girl flung money all about the stage in a magnificently scornful gesture. Which led us on to the large number of plays and novels there are where money is trampled on, burned, flung about or otherwise ritually scorned; which is odd, since such gestures never take place in life. Not at all, said a matron from New York—she had seen with her own eyes some Flower Children burning money on a sidewalk to show their contempt for it; but for her part what it showed was that they must have rich parents. (This dates the story, or at least the fog.)

All the same, considering the role money plays in all our lives, it *is* odd how often authors cause characters to insult dollar bills, rubles, pound notes. Which enables audience, readers, to go home, or to shut the book, feeling cleansed of the stuff? Above it?

Whereas we are told that in less surly days sultans on feast days flung gold coins into crowds happy to scramble for it; that kings caused showers of gold to descend on loved ministers; and that if jewels fell in showers from the sky no one would dream of asking suspicious questions.

The nearest any one of us could remember to this kingly stuff was a certain newspaper mogul in London who would reward a promising young journalist for an article which he (the mogul) liked, with an envelope stuffed full of five pound notes sent around by special messenger—but this kind of thing is only too open to unkind interpretation, and the amount of illfeeling aroused in the bosoms of fellow journalists, and the terror in that of the recipient for fear the thing might get talked about, is probably why we stage such scenes as it were in reverse, and why, on the edge of a magic fountain, we slide in a single coin, like a love letter into an envelope during an affair which one's better sense entirely deplores. Sympathetic magic—but a small magic, a mini-magic, a most furtive summoning of the Gods of Gold. And, if a hand rose from the fountain to throw us coins and jewels, it is more than likely that, schooled as we are by recent literature, we'd sneer and throw them back in its teeth—so to speak.

And now a man who had not spoken at all said that he knew of a case where jewels had been flung into the dust of a public square in Italy. No one had thrown them back. He took from his pocket a wallet, and from the wallet a fold of paper such as jewellers use, and on the paper lay a single spark or gleam of light. It was a slice of milk-and-rainbow opal. Yes, he said, he had been there. He had picked up the fragment and kept it. It wasn't valuable, of course. He would tell us the story if he thought there was time, but for some reason it was a tale so precious to him that he didn't want to bungle it through having to hurry. Here there was another swirl of silkily gleaming fog beyond the glass of the restaurant wall, and another announcement of un-avoidable delay.

So he told the story. One day someone will intro-duce me to a young man called Nikki (perhaps, or what you will) who was born during the Second World War in Italy. His father was a hero, and his mother now the wife of the Ambassador to.... Or perhaps in a bus, or at a dinner party, there will be a girl who has a pearl hanging around her neck on a chain, and when asked about it she will say: Imagine, my mother was given this pearl by a man who was practically a stranger, and when she gave it to me she said. . . . Something like that will happen: and then this story will have a different beginning, not a fog at all . . . .

There was a man called Ephraim who lived in Johannesburg. His father was to do with diamonds, as had been his father. The family were immigrants. This is still true of all people from Johannesburg, a city a century old. Ephraim was a middle son, not brilliant or stupid, not good or bad. He was nothing in particular. His brothers became diamond merchants, but Ephraim was not cut out for anything immediately obvious, and so at last he was apprenticed to an uncle to learn the trade of diamond cutting.

To cut a diamond perfectly is an act like a samurai's sword-thrust, or a master archer's centred arrow. When an important diamond is shaped a man may spend a week, or even weeks, studying it, accumulating powers of attention, memory, intuition, till he has reached that moment when he finally knows that a tap, no more, at just *that* point of tension in the stone will split it exactly *so*.

While Ephraim learned to do this, he lived at home in a Johannesburg suburb; and his brothers and sisters married and had families. He was the son who took his time about getting married, and about whom the family first joked, saying that he was choosy; and then they remained silent when others talked of him with that edge on their voices, irritated, a little malicious, even frightened, which is caused by those men and women who refuse to fulfil the ordinary purposes of nature. The kind ones said he was a good son, working nicely under his uncle Ben, and living respectably at home, and on Sunday nights playing poker with bachelor friends. He was twenty-five, then thirty, thirty-five, forty. His parents became old and died, and he lived alone in the family house. People stopped noticing him. Nothing was expected of him.

Then a senior person became ill, and Ephraim was asked to fly in his stead to Alexandria for a special job. A certain rich merchant of Alexandria had purchased an uncut diamond as a present for his daughter, who was shortly to be married. He wished only the best for the diamond. Ephraim, revealed by this happening as one of the world's master diamond cutters, flew to Egypt, spent some days in communion with the stone in a quiet room in the merchant's house, and then caused it to fall apart into three lovely pieces. These were for a ring and earrings.

Now he should have flown home again; but the merchant asked him to dinner. An odd chance that —unusual. Not many people got inside that rich closed world. But perhaps the merchant had become infected by the week of rising tension while Ephraim became one with the diamond in a quiet room.

At dinner Ephraim met the girl for whom the jewels were destined.

And now—but what can be said about the fortnight that followed? Certainly not that Ephraim, the little artisan from Johannesburg, fell in love with Mihrène, daughter of a modern merchant prince. Nothing so simple. And that the affair had about it a quality out of the ordinary was shown by the reaction of the merchant himself, Mihrène's conventional papa.

Conventional, commonplace, banal—these are the words for the members of the set, or class to which Mihrène Kantannis belonged. In all the cities about the Mediterranean they live in a scattered community, very rich, but tastefully so, following international fashions, approving Paris when they should and London when they should, making trips to New York or Rome, summering on whichever shore they have chosen, by a kind of group instinct, to be the right one for the year, and sharing comfortably tolerant opinions. They were people, are people, with nothing remarkable about them but their wealth, and the enchanting Mihrène, whom

Ephraim first saw in a mist of white embroidered muslin standing by a fountain, was a girl neither more pretty nor more gifted than, let's say, a dozen that evening in Alexandria, a thousand or so in Egypt, hundreds of thousands in the countries round about all of which produce so plentifully her particular type—her beautiful type: small-boned, black-haired, black-eyed, apricot-skinned, lithe.

She had lived for twenty years in this atmosphere of well chosen luxury; loved and bickered with her mother and her sisters; respected her papa; and was intending to marry Paulo, a young man from South America with whom she would continue to live exactly the same kind of life, only in Buenos Aires.

For her it was an ordinary evening, a family dinner at which a friend of papa's was present. She did not know about the diamonds: they were to be a surprise. She was wearing last year's dress and a choker of false pearls: that season it was smart to wear "costume" pearls, and to leave one's real pearls in a box on one's dressing-table.

Ephraim, son of jewellers, saw the false pearls around that neck and suffered.

Why, though? Johannesburg is full of pretty girls.

But he had not travelled much, and Johannesburg, rough, built on gold, as it were breathing by the power of gold, a city waxing and waning with the fortunes of gold (as befits this story) may be exciting, violent, vibrant, but it has no mystery, nothing for the imagination, no invisible dimensions. Whereas Alexandria . . . this house, for instance, with its discreetly blank outer walls that might conceal anything, crime, or the hidden court of an exiled king, held inner gardens and fountains, and Mihrène, dressed appropriately in moonwhite and who . . . well, perhaps she wasn't entirely at her best that evening. There were those who said she had an ugly laugh. Sometimes the family joked that it was lucky she would never have to earn a living. At one point during dinner, perhaps feeling that she ought to contribute to the entertainment, she told a rather flat and slightly bitchy story about a friend. She was certainly bored, yawned once or twice, and did not try too hard to hide the yawns. The diamond cutter from Johannesburg gazed at her, forgot to eat, and asked twice why she wore false pearls in a voice rough with complaint. He was gauche, she decided —and forgot him.

He did not return home, but wired for money. He had never spent any, and so had a great deal available for the single perfect pearl which he spent days looking for, and which he found at last in a back room in Cairo, where he sat bargaining over coffee cups for some days with an old Persian dealer who knew as much about gems as he did, and who would not trade in anything but the best.

With this jewel he arrived at the house of Mihrène's father, and when he was seated in a room opening on to an inner court where jasmine clothed a wall, and lily pads a pool, he asked permission to give the pearl to the young girl.

It had been strange that papa had invited this tradesman to dinner. It was strange that now papa did not get angry. He was shrewd: it was his life to be shrewd. There was no nuance of commercial implication in a glance, a tone of voice, a turn of phrase that he was not certain to assess rightly. Opposite this fabulously rich man into whose house only the rich came as guests, sat a little diamond cutter who proposed to give his daughter a small fortune in the shape of a pearl, and who wanted nothing in return for it.

They drank coffee, and then they drank whisky, and they talked of the world's jewels and of the forthcoming wedding, until for the second time Ephraim was asked to dinner.

At dinner Mihrène sat opposite the elderly gentleman (he was forty-five or so) who was papa's business friend, and was ordinarily polite: then slightly more polite, because of a look from papa. The party was Mihrène, her father, her fiancé Paulo, and Ephraim. The mother and sisters were visiting elsewhere. Nothing happened during the meal. The young couple were rather inattentive to the older pair. At the end, Ephraim took a screw of paper from his pocket, and emptied from it a single perfect pearl that had a gleam like the flesh of a rose, or of a twenty-year-old girl. This pearl he offered to Mihrène, with the remark that she oughtn't to wear false pearls. Again it was harshly inflected; a complaint, or a reproach for imperfect perfection.

The pearl lay on white damask in candlelight. Into the light above the pearl was thrust the face of Ephraim, whose features she could reconstruct from the last time she had seen him a couple of weeks before only with the greatest of difficulty.

It was, of course, an extraordinary moment. But not dramatic—no, it lacked that high apex of decisiveness as when Ephraim tapped a diamond, or an archer lets loose his bow. Mihrène looked at her father for an explanation. So, of course, did her fiancé. Her father did not look confused, or embarrassed, so much as that he wore the air of somebody standing on one side because here is a situation which he has never professed himself competent to judge. And Mihrène had probably never before in her life been left free to make a decision.

She picked up the pearl from the damask, and let it lie in her palm. She, her fiancé, and her father, looked at the pearl whose value they were all well-equipped to assess, and Ephraim looked sternly at the girl. Then she lifted long, feathery black lashes and looked at him—in enquiry? An appeal to be let off? His eyes were judging, disappointed; they said what his words had said: Why are you content with the secondrate?

Preposterous . . .

Impossible . . .

Finally Mihrène gave the slightest shrug of shoulders tonight covered in pink organza, and said to

Ephraim, Thank you, Thank you very much.

They rose from the table. The four drank coffee on the terrace over which rose a wildly evocative Alexandrian moon, two nights away from the full, a moon quite unlike any that might shine over strident Johannesburg. Mihrène let the pearl lie on her palm and reflect moonrays, while from time to time her black eyes engaged with Ephraim's—but what colour his were had never been, would never be, of interest to anyone—and, there was no doubt of it, he was like someone warning, or reminding, or even threatening.

Next day he went back to Johannesburg, and on Mihrène's dressing-table lay a small silver box in which was a single perfect pearl.

She was to marry in three weeks.

Immediately the incident became in the family: "That crazy little Jew who fell for Mihrène. . . ." Her acceptance of the pearl was talked of as an act of delicacy on her part, of kindness. "Mihrène was so kind to the poor old thing . . . ." Thus they smoothed over what had happened, made acceptable an incident which could have no place in their life, their thinking. But they knew, of course, and most particularly did Mihrène know, that something else had happened.

When she refused to marry Paulo, quite prettily and nicely, papa and mamma Kantannis made ritual remarks about her folly, her ingratitude, and so forth, but in engagements like these no hearts are expected to be broken, for the marriages are like the arranged marriages of dynasties. If she did not marry Paulo, she would marry someone like him—and she was very young.

They remarked that she had not been herself since the affair of the pearl. Papa said to himself that he would see to it no more fly-by-nights arrived at his dinner table. They arranged for Mihrène a visit to cousins in Istanbul.

Meanwhile in Johannesburg a diamond cutter worked at his trade, cutting diamonds for engagement rings, dress rings, tie pins, necklaces, bracelets. He imagined a flat bowl of crystal, which glittered like diamonds, in which were massed roses. But the roses were all white, shades of white. He saw roses which were cold marble white, white verging on coffee colour, greenish white, like the wings of certain butterflies, white that blushed, a creamy white,

white that was nearly beige, white that was almost yellow. He imagined a hundred shades of white in rose shapes. These he pressed together, filled a crystal dish with them and gave them to—Mihrène? It is possible that already he scarcely thought of her. He imagined how he would collect stones in shades of white, and create a perfect jewel, bracelet, necklet, or crescent for the hair, and present this jewel to —Mihrène? Does it matter whom it was for? He bought opals, like mist held behind glass on which lights moved and faded, like milk where fire lay buried, like the congealed breath of a girl on a frosty night. He bought pearls, each one separately, each one perfect. He bought fragments of mother-of-pearl. He bought moonstones like clouded diamonds. He even bought lumps of glass that someone had shaped to reflect light perfectly. He bought white jade and crystals and collected chips of diamond to make the suppressed fires in pearl and opal flash out in reply to their glittering frost. These jewels he had in folded flat paper, and they were kept first in a small cigarette box, and then were transferred to a larger box that had been for throat lozenges, and then to an even larger box that held cigars. He played with these gems, dreamed over them, arranged them in his mind in a thousand ways. Sometimes he remembered an exquisite girl dressed in moonmist: the memory was becoming more and more like a sentimental postcard or an oldfashioned calendar.

In Istanbul Mihrène married, without her family's approval, a young Italian engineer whom normally she would never have met. Her uncle was engaged in reconstructing a certain yacht; the engineer was in the uncle's office to discuss the reconstruction when Mihrène came in. It was she who made the first move: it would have to be. He was twenty-seven, with nothing but his salary, and no particular prospects. His name was Carlos. He was political. That is, precisely, he was revolutionary, a conspirator. Politics did not enter the world of Mihrène. Or rather, it could be said that such families *are* politics, politics in their aspect of wealth, but this only becomes evident when deals are made that are so vast that they have international cachet, and repute, like the alliances or rifts between countries.

Carlos called Mihrène "a white goose" when she tried to impress him with her seriousness. He called her "a little rich bitch." He made a favour of taking her to meetings where desperately serious young men and women discussed the forthcoming war— the year was 1939. It was an affair absolutely within the traditions of such romances: her family were bound to think she was throwing herself away; he and his friends on the whole considered that it was he who was conferring benefits.

To give herself courage in her determination to be worthy of this young hero, she would open a tiny silver box where a pearl lay on silk, and say to herself: *He* thought I was worth something. . . .

She married her Carlos in the week Paulo married a girl from a French dynasty. Mihrène went to Rome and lived in a small villa without servants, and with nothing to fall back on but the memory of a nondescript elderly man who had sat opposite her throughout two long dull dinners and who had given her a pearl as if he were giving her a lesson. She thought that in all her life no one else had ever demanded anything of her, ever asked anything, ever taken her seriously.

The war began. In Buenos Aires the bride who had taken her place lived in luxury. Mihrène, a poor housewife, saw her husband who was a conspirator against the fascist Mussolini, become a conscript in Mussolini's armies, then saw him go away to fight, while she waited for the birth of her first child.

The war swallowed her. When she was heard of again, her hero was dead, and her first child was dead, and her second, conceived on Carlos' final leave, was due to be born in a couple of months. She was in a small town in the centre of Italy with no resources at all but her pride: she had sworn she would not earn the approval of her parents on any terms but her own. The family she had married into had suffered badly: she had a room in the house of an aunt.

The Germans were retreating through Italy: after them chased the victorious armies of the Allies . . . but that sounds like an official war history.

To try again: over a peninsula that was shattered, ruinous, starved by war, two armies of men foreign to the natives of the place, were in movement; one in retreat up towards the body of Europe, the other following it. There were places where these opposing bodies were geographically so intermingled that only uniforms distinguished them. Both armies were warm, well-clothed, well-fed, supplied with alcohol and cigarettes. The native inhabitants had no heat, no warm clothes, little food, no cigarettes. They had, however, a great deal of alcohol.

In one army was a man called Ephraim who, being elderly, was not a combatant, but part of the machinery which supplied it with food and goods. He was a sergeant, and as unremarkable in the army as he was in civilian life. For the four years he had been a soldier, for the most part in North Africa, he had pursued a private interest, or obsession, which was, when he arrived anywhere at all, to seek out the people and places that could add yet another fragment of iridescent or gleaming substance to the mass which he carried around in a flat tin in his pack.

The men he served with found him and his preoccupation mildly humorous. He was not disliked or liked enough to make a target for that concentration of unease caused by people who alarm others. They did not laugh at him, or call him madman. Perhaps he was more like that dog who is a regiment's pet. Once he mislaid his tin of loot and a couple of men went into a moderate danger to get it back: sometimes a comrade would bring him a bit of something or other picked up in a bazaar—amber, an amulet, a jade. He advised them how to make bargains; he went on expeditions with them to buy stones for wives and girls back home.

He was in Italy that week when—*everything disintegrated*. Anyone who has been in, or near, war (which means, by now, everyone, or at least everyone in Europe and Asia) knows that time—a week, days, sometimes hours—when everything falls apart, when all forms of order dissolve, including those which mark the difference between enemy and enemy.

During this time old scores of all kinds are settled. It is when unpopular officers get killed by "accident." It is when a man who has an antipathy for another will kill him, or beat him up. A man who wants a woman will rape her, if she is around, or rape another in her stead if she is not. Women get raped; and those who want to be will make sure they are where the raping is. A woman who hates another will harm her. In short, it is a time of anarchy, of looting, of arson and destruction for destruction's sake. There are those who believe that this time out of ordinary order is the reason for war, its hidden justification, its purpose and law, another pattern behind the one we see. Afterwards there are no records of what has happened. There is no one to keep records: everyone is engaged in participating, or in protecting himself.

Ephraim was in a small town near Florence when his war reached that phase. There was a certain corporal, also from Johannesburg, who always had a glitter in his look when they talked of Ephraim's tin full of jewels. On an evening when every human being in the place was hunter or hunted, manoeuvred for advantage, or followed scents of gain, this man, in civilian life a store keeper, looked across a room at Ephraim and grinned. Ephraim knew what to expect. Everyone knew what to expect—at such moments much older knowledges come to the surface together with old instincts. Ephraim quietly left a schoolroom for that week converted into a mess, and went out into the early dark of streets emptied by fear, where walls still shook and dust fell in clouds because of near gunfire. But it was also very quiet. Terror's cold nausea silences, places invisible hands across mouths.... The occasional person hurrying through these streets kept his eyes in front, and his mouth tight. Two such people meeting did not look at each other except for a moment when their eyes violently encountered in a hard clash of enquiry. Behind every shutter or pane or door people stood or sat or crouched, waiting for the time out of order to end, and guns and sharp instruments stood near their hands.

Through these streets went Ephraim. The Corporal had not seen him go, but by now would certainly have found the scent. At any moment he would catch up with Ephraim who carried in his hand a flat tin, and who as he walked looked into holes in walls and in pavements, peered into a church half filled with rubble, investigated torn earth where bomb fragments had fallen and even looked up into the branches of trees as he passed and at the plants growing at doorways. Finally as he passed a fountain clogged with debris he knelt for a moment and slid his tin down into the mud. He walked away, fast, not looking back to see if he had been seen, and around the corner of the church he met Corporal Van der Merwe. As Ephraim came up to his enemy he held out empty hands and stood still. The Corporal was a big man and twenty years younger. Van der Merwe gave him a frowning look, indicative of his powers of shrewd assessment, rather like Mihrène's father's look when he heard how this little nonentity proposed to give his daughter a valuable pearl for no reason at all, and when Ephraim saw it, he at once raised his hands above his head like a prisoner surrendering, while Van der Merwe frisked him. There was a moment when Ephraim might very well have been killed: it hung in the balance. But down the street a rabble of soldiers were looting pictures and valuables from another church, and Van der Merwe, his attention caught by them, simply watched Ephraim walk away, and then ran off himself to join the looters.

By the time that season of anarchy had finished, Ephraim was a couple of hundred miles north. Six months later, in a town ten miles from the one where he had nearly been murdered by a man once again his military subordinate (but that incident had disappeared, had become buried in the foreign texture of another time, or dimension), Ephraim asked for an evening's leave and travelled as he could to V.... where he imagined, perhaps, that he would walk through deserted streets to a rubble-filled fountain and beside this fountain would kneel, and slide his hand into dirty water to retrieve his treasure.

But the square was full of people, and though this was not a time when a cafe served more than a cup of bad coffee or water flavoured with chemicals, the two cafes had people in them who were half starved but already inhabiting the forms of ordinary life. They served, of course, unlimited quantities of cheap wine. Everyone was drunk, or tipsy. In a wine country, when there is no food, wine becomes a kind of food, craved like food. Ephraim walked past the fountain and saw that the water was filthy, too dirty to let anyone see what was in it, and whether it had been cleared of rubble, and, with the rubble, his treasure.

He sat on the pavement under a torn awning, by a cracked wood table, and ordered coffee. He was the only soldier there; or at least, the only uniform. The main tide of soldiery was washing back and forth to one side of this little town. Uniforms meant barter, meant food, clothing, cigarettes. In a moment half a dozen little boys were at his elbow offering him girls. Women of all ages were sauntering past or making themselves visible, or trying to catch his eye, since the female population of the town were for the most part in that condition for which in our debased time we have the shorthand term: being prepared to sell themselves for a cigarette. Old women, old men, cripples, all kinds of persons, stretched in front of him hands displaying various more or less useless objects—lighters, watches, old buckles or bottles or brooches—hoping to get chocolate or food in return. Ephraim sat on, sad with himself because he had not brought eggs or tinned stuffs or chocolate. He had not thought of it. He sat while hungry people with sharp faces that glittered with a winy fever pressed about him and the bodies of a dozen or so women arranged themselves in this or that pose for his inspection. He felt ashamed. He felt sick. He was almost ready to go away and forget his tin full of gems. Then a tired-looking woman in a much-washed print dress lifted high in front because of pregnancy came to sit at his table. He thought she was there to sell herself, and hardly looked at her, unable to bear it that a pregnant woman was brought to such a pass.

She said: "Don't you remember me?"

And now he searched her face, and she searched

his. He looked for Mihrène; and she tried to see in him what it was that changed her life, to find out what it was that pearl embodied which she carried with her in a bit of cloth sewn into her slip.

They sat trying to exchange news; but these two people had so little in common they could not even say: And how is so and so? What has happened to him, or to her?

The hungry inhabitants of the town withdrew a little way, because this soldier had become a person, a man who was a friend of Mihrène, who was their friend.

The two were there for a couple of hours. They were on the whole more embarrassed than anything. It was clear to both by now that whatever events had taken place between them, momentous or not (they are not equipped to say) these events were in some realm or on a level where their daylight selves were strangers. It was certainly not the point that she, the unforgettable girl of Alexandria had become a rather drab young woman waiting to give birth in a war-shattered town; not the point that for her he had carried with him for four years of war a treasury of gems some precious, some mildly valuable, some worthless, bits of substance with one thing in common: their value related to some other good which had had, arbitrarily and for a short time, the name *Mihrène*.

It had become intolerable to sit there, over coffee made of burned grain, while all round great hungry eyes focussed on him, the soldier, who had come so cruelly to their starving town with empty hands. He had soon to leave. He had reached this town on the back boards of a peasant's cart, there being no other transport; and if he did not get another lift of the same kind, he would have to walk ten miles before midnight.

Over the square was rising a famished watery moon, unlike the moons of his own city, unlike the wild moons of Egypt. At last he simply got up and walked to the edge of the evil-smelling fountain. He kneeled down on its edge, plunged in his hand, encountered all sorts of slimy things, probably dead rats or cats or even bits of dead people, and after some groping felt the familiar shape of his tin. He pulled it out, wiped it dry on some old newspaper that had blown there, went back to the table, sat down, opened the tin. Pearls are fed on light and air. Opals don't like being shut away from light which makes their depths come alive. But no water had got in, and he emptied the glittering gleaming heap on to the cracked wood of the table top.

All round pressed the hungry people who looked at the gems and thought of food.

She took from her breast a bit of cloth and untwisted her pearl. She held it out to him.

"I never sold it," she said.

And now he looked at her—sternly, as he had done before.

She said, in the pretty English of those who have learned it from governesses: "I have sometimes needed food, I've been hungry, you know! I've had no servants . . . ."

He looked at her. Oh, how she knew that look, how she had studied it in memory! Irritation, annoyance, grief. All these, but above all disappointment. And more than these, a warning, or reminder. It said, she felt: Silly white goose! Rich little bitch! Poor little nothing! Why do you always get it wrong? Why are you stupid? What is a pearl compared with what it stands for? If you are hungry and need money, sell it, of course!

She sat in that sudden stillness that says a person is fighting not to weep. Her beautiful eyes brimmed. Then she said stubbornly: "I'll never sell it. Never!"

As for him he was muttering: I should have brought food. I was a *dummkopf*. What's the use of these things. . . .

But in the hungry eyes around him he read that they were thinking how even in times of famine there are always men and women who have food hidden away to be bought by gold or jewels.

"Take them," he said to the children, to the women, to the old people.

They did not understand him, did not believe him.

He said again: "Go on. Take them!"

No one moved. Then he stood up and began flinging into the air pearls, opals, moonstones, gems of all kinds, to fall as they would. For a few moments there was a mad scene of people bobbing and scrambling, and the square emptied as people raced back to the corners they lived in with what they had picked up out of the dust. It was not yet time for the myth to start, the story of how a soldier had walked into the town, and inexplicably pulled treasure out of the fountain which he flung into the air like a king or a sultan—treasure that was ambiguous and fertile like a king's, since one man might pick up the glitter of a diamond that later turned out to be worthless glass, and another be left with a smallish pearl that had nevertheless been so carefully chosen it was worth months of food, or even a house or small farm.

"I must go," said Ephraim to his companion.

She inclined her head in farewell, as to an acquaintance re-encountered. She watched a greying dumpy little man walk away past a fountain, past a church, then out of sight.

Later that night she took out the pearl and held it in her hand. If she sold it, she would remain comfortably independent of her own family. Here, in the circle of the family of her dead husband, she would marry again, another engineer or civil servant: she would be worth marrying, even as a widow with a child. Of course if she returned to her own family, she would also marry, as a rich young widow with a small child from that dreadful war, luckily now over.

Such thoughts went through her head: at last she thought that it didn't make any difference what she did. Whatever function Ephraim's intervention had performed in her life, was over when she refused to marry Paulo, had married Carlos, had come to Italy and given birth to two children, one dead from an unimportant children's disease that had been fatal only because of the quality of war-food, war-warmth. She had been wrenched out of her pattern, had been stamped, or claimed by the pearl—by something else. Nothing she could do now would put her back where she had been. It did not matter whether she stayed in Italy or returned to the circles she had been born in.

As for Ephraim he went back to Johannesburg when the war finished, and continued to cut diamonds and to play poker on Sunday nights.

This story ended more or less with the calling of the flight number. As we went to the tarmac where illuminated wisps of fog still lingered, the lady from Texas asked the man who had told the story if perhaps he was Ephraim?

"No," said Dr. Rosen, a man of sixty or so from

Johannesburg, a brisk welldressed man with nothing much to notice about him—like most of the world's citizens.

No, he was most emphatically not Ephraim.

Then how did he know all this? Perhaps he was there?

Yes, he was there. But if he was to tell us how he came to be a hundred miles from where he should have been, in that chaotic, horrible week—it was horrible, horrible!—and in civvies, then that story would be even longer than the one he had already told us.

Couldn't he tell us why he was there?

Perhaps he was after that tin of Ephraim's too! We could think so if we liked. It would be excusable of us to think so. There was a fortune in that tin, and everyone in the regiment knew it.

He was a friend of Ephraim's then? He knew Ephraim?

Yes, he could say that. He had known Ephraim for, let's see, nearly fifty years. Yes, he thought he could say he was Ephraim's friend.

In the aircraft Dr. Rosen sat reading, with nothing more to tell us.

ON INTELLIGENCE

Paul Valéry

THE MACHINE RULES. Human life is rigorously controlled by it, dominated by the terribly precise will of mechanisms. These creatures of man are exacting. They are now reacting on their creators, making them like themselves. They want well-trained humans; they are gradually wiping out the differences between men, fitting them into their own orderly functioning, into the uniformity of their own regimes. They are thus shaping humanity for their own use, almost in their own image.

There is a sort of pact between the machine and ourselves, like the terrible contract between the nervous system and the subtle demon of drugs. The more useful the machine seems to us, the more it becomes so; and the more it becomes so, the more *incomplete* we are, the more incapable of doing without it. There is such a thing as *the reciprocal* of the useful.

The most redoubtable machines, perhaps, are not those that revolve or run, to transport or transform matter or energy. There are other kinds, not built of copper or steel but of narrowly specialized individuals: I refer to organizations, those administrative machines constructed in imitation of the *impersonal aspects* of the mind.

Civilization is measured by the increasing size and number of such structures. They may be likened to huge human beings, barely conscious, hardly able to feel at all, but endowed to excess with all the elementary and regular functions of an inordinately oversized nervous system. Everything in them having to do with relations, transmission, agreement, and correspondence, is magnified to the monstrous scale of *one man per cell*. They are endowed with a limitless memory, as fragile as the fiber of paper. That is where they get all their reflexes, which are laws, regulations, statutes, precedents. Not a single mortal is left unswallowed into the structure of these machines, to become an object of their functioning, a non-descript element in their cycles. The life or death, the pleasures and works of men are details, means, incidents in the activity of these beings, whose rule is tempered only by the war they wage against each other.

Each of us is a cog in one of these groups, or rather we belong to several different groups at once, surrendering to each of them a part of our self-ownership, and taking from each a part of our social definition and our license to exist. We are all citizens, soldiers, taxpayers, men of a certain trade, supporters of a certain party, adherents of a certain religion, members of a certain organization, a certain club.

To be a member . . . is a remarkable expression. As a result of the more and more precise and minute analysis and carving up of the human mass, we have become somehow quite well-defined entities. As such, we are now no more than objects of speculation, veritable *things*. Here I must utter certain awkward words; I am obliged, though with a shudder, to say that *irresponsibility*, *interchangeability*, *interdependence*, and *uniformity*, in customs, manners, and even in dreams, are overtaking the human race. It seems that the sexes themselves are bound to become indistinguishable except in anatomical characteristics.

All the foregoing remarks must now be brought together and related to our idea of *intelligence as a faculty*, and we must ask ourselves whether our regime of intense and frequent stimulants, disguised forms of punishment, oppressive utilities, systematic surprises, overorganized facilities and enjoyments is not bound to bring on a kind of permanent deformation of the mind, the loss of certain characteristics and the acquisition of certain others; and whether, in particular, those very talents which have made us desire all this *progress*, as a means of employing and developing themselves, will not be affected by abuse, degraded by their own handiwork, and exhausted by their own activity.

Among living intellects, some spend themselves in serving the machine, others in building it, others in inventing or planning a more powerful type; a final category of intellects spend themselves in trying to escape its domination. These rebellious minds feel with a shudder that the once complete and autonomous *whole* that was the soul of ancient man is now becoming some inferior kind of *daemon* that wishes only to collaborate, to join the crowd, to find security in being dependent and happiness in a closed system that will be all the more closed as man makes it more closely suited to man. But *this is to give a new definition of man.*

The whole disturbance in our minds today shows that great changes are coming in our idea of ourselves. . . .

Our civilization is taking on, or tending to take on, the structure and properties of a machine, as I indicated just now. This machine will not tolerate less than world-wide rule; it will not allow a single human being to survive outside its control, uninvolved in its functioning. Furthermore, it cannot put up with ill-defined lives within its sphere of operation. Its precision, which is its essence, cannot endure vagueness or social caprice; irregular situations are incompatible with good running order. *It cannot put up with anyone whose duties and circumstances are not precisely specified.* It tends to eliminate those individuals who from its own point of view do not exactly fit, and to reclassify the rest without regard to the past or even the future of the species.

It has already begun to attack the ill-organized populations of the earth. Moreover, there is a law (a corollary of that primitive law which turns need and the sense of power into aggressive impulses) decreeing that the highly organized must invariably take the offensive against the poorly organized.

The machine—that is, the Western World—could not help turning, one day, against those ill-defined and sometimes *incommensurable* men inside it.

So we are witnessing an attack on the indefinable mass by the will or the necessity for *definition*. Fiscal laws, economic laws, the regulation of labor, and, above all, the profound changes in general technology . . . everything is used for counting, assimilating, leveling, bracketing, and arranging that group of indefinables, those *natural solitaries* who constitute a part of the intellectual population. The rest, more easily absorbed, will inevitably be redefined and reclassified.

A few remarks will perhaps clarify what I have just written.

It was never more than indirectly that society could afford the life of a poet, a thinker, an artist, whose works were unhurried and profound. It sometimes uses them as fake servants or nominal functionaries—professors, curators, librarians. But the professions are complaining; every government official's small freedom of decision is being more and more reduced; there is less and less *play* in the machine.

The machine neither will nor can recognize any but "professionals."

How is it to go about reducing everyone to professionals?

There is a world of fumbling involved in trying to determine the characteristics of those who specialize in the intellect!

Each of us uses whatever mind he has. An unskilled laborer uses his, *from his own point of view*, just as much as anyone else, a philosopher or a mathematician. If his speech seems crude and simple-minded to us, ours is strange and absurd to him, and everyone is an unskilled laborer to someone else.

How could it be otherwise? Besides, every man

dreams at times, or gets drunk, or both; and in his sleep as in his cups, the ferment of images and their free and *useless* combinations make him a Shakespeare—to what degree is unknown and unknowable. And our laborer, stunned by fatigue or alcohol, becomes the playground of spirits.

But, you will say, *he does not know how to use them.*

Which simply means that he is a laborer from our point of view, though a Shakespeare from his own. When he wakes, all he lacks is knowing the name of Shakespeare and some notion of literature. He is unaware of himself as a creator.

And who would dare put, or not put, a fortune teller, a master of ceremonies, or a circus clown in the category of intellectuals?

Who will maintain that more intelligence is expended in one head than another; that more intelligence and more knowledge are needed in teaching than in business speculations or in creating an industry?

We must make up our minds to dabble in examples. While dabbling we sometimes splash up a few drops of light.

In questions that are by nature confused, and are

so for everybody, I find it permissible—perhaps laudable—to present, just as they are, the tentative efforts, the half-formed notions, and even the rejected and refuted phases of one's thought.

I have sometimes seen very surprising definitions of the intellectual. Some include the accountant and exclude the poet. Some, if taken quite literally, are so inclusive that they are unable to exclude those beautiful machines so clever at making calculations or squaring curves, and far superior to many brains.

Suppose (and this supposition is not mine; it was made, I think, by an English or an American writer whose name I have forgotten, and whose book I have not read; I am merely borrowing the idea, which I found a long time ago in some review of the book) . . . well, the author in question supposes that a kind of mysterious disease attacks and quickly destroys all the paper in the world. No defense, no remedy; it is impossible to find any means of exterminating the microbe or of countering the physiochemical phenomenon attacking the cellulose. The unknown destroyer penetrates drawers and chests, reduces to dust the contents of our pocketbooks and our libraries; every written thing vanishes.

Paper, you know, plays the part of a storage battery and a conductor; it conducts not only from one man to another but from one time to another, carrying a *highly variable charge of authenticity or credibility.*

Imagine, then, that paper is no more: no more bank notes, bonds, treaties, records, laws, poems, newspapers, etc. At once the whole life of society is struck down, and out of the ruins of the past we see the future emerging, the potential and the probable —*pure reality.*

Everyone immediately realizes that he is reduced to his own sphere of perception and action. In each individual future and past draw incredibly close together; we are reduced to the radius of our senses and our immediate acts.

It is easy to imagine this example of the enormous role played by verbal and fiduciary values. Nothing could more impress upon us the fragility of world order and the *spiritual nature* of social order than this fantastic supposition.

But I shall now make another, a far less fantastic

supposition, which ought on that account to be more impressive: instead of decaying from some disease, a sort of tuberculosis of paper (that fragile basis of so many things), suppose now that the *basis of that basis* should weaken and collapse—I mean the trust, the confidence, the credit we give to written paper, thus giving it all its value. Such a thing has happened before, but never to the universal extent we must unhappily recognize in our day. We are no longer in the realm of supposition. We have seen solemn treaties trampled under foot, others shorn of all force in a day; States, *all States*, are seen to fail in their obligations, to repudiate their signatures, to threaten or repay their creditors with the "abhorred vacuum."

We have seen legislators constrained to release individuals themselves from obligations imposed on them by private contracts.

I make so bold as to say—an extraordinary thing! —that gold itself, *gold* is no longer fully possessed of its immemorial and mythical sovereignty; yet once it seemed to contain within its precious and weighty atom the refined essence of confidence! . . .

What we have, then, is a general crisis of values.

Nothing escapes, either in the economic or the moral or the political realm. Freedom itself has ceased to be fashionable. Even the most up-to-date opinions, which used to clamor for it furiously fifty years ago, today deny and immolate it! . . . The crisis is spreading to everything: science, civil law, Newton's mechanics, diplomatic traditions. Everything is affected by it. I am not even sure that love itself is not coming to be evaluated in a very different way from that of the last half-dozen centuries . . . .

In short, a crisis of confidence, of fundamental conceptions—there is indeed, a crisis of all human relationships, that is to say, of the values given or received by minds.

But that is not yet all; we must now envisage (and it is with this that I shall end) a crisis of the mind itself. I shall not speak of the particular crisis in the sciences, which seem now to despair of their ancient ideal of explaining the universe as a unified whole. The universe is breaking up, losing all hope of a single design. The world of the ultramicroscopic seems strangely different from the world as an agglomerate mass; in the former, even the identity of bodies is lost . . . . Nor shall I mention the crisis of determinism, that is to say, of causality.

I am thinking, rather, of the dangers that are so seriously threatening the very existence of all the higher values of the mind.

It is clearly possible to conceive an almost happy condition for humanity, or at least a stable, pacified, organized, comfortable condition (I do not say that we are anywhere near it); but in conceiving such a state, we realize that it brings with it, or would bring, a most tepid intellectual temperature: in general, *happy peoples have no mind*. They have no great need of it.

If, then, the world is moving down a certain incline and has already gone some distance down it, we must from now on *recognize that the conditions are rapidly vanishing in which and thanks to which the things we most admire, man's most admirable works so far, have been created and had their influence.*

Everything now conspires against the chances of creating what might be, or rather might have been, noblest and most beautiful. How can this be?

To begin with, it is easy to observe in ourselves a diminution, a kind of general clouding over of sensibility. We moderns are not very sensitive. Modern man has blunted his senses; he puts up with every kind of noise, as we all know; he puts up with nauseating smells, with violently contrasting or insanely intense lighting; he is subjected to perpetual vibration; he feels the need of brutal stimulants, strident sounds, the strongest drinks, brief and bestial emotions.

He tolerates incoherence, he lives in mental disorder. On the other hand, the work of the mind to which we owe everything has become sometimes too facile. Co-ordinated mental effort is today equipped with powerful instruments to make it easier, sometimes to the point of doing away with it. We have invented symbols and built machines to save attention, to relieve us of the patient and difficult labor of the mind; and such methods of symbolization and rapid depiction can only continue to multiply. *Their aim is to do away with the effort of thinking.*

Finally, the conditions of modern life tend inevitably, implacably, to make individuals all alike, to level character; and, unhappily yet necessarily, the average tends to decline *toward the lowest type*. Bad money drives out good.

Another danger: I notice that credulity and naïveté are developing to an alarming degree. I have noticed in the last few years a number of new superstitions that were nonexistent in France twenty years ago and now are gradually coming even into our drawing rooms. We see very distinguished people knocking on wood and practicing other exorcisms and fiduciary acts. Moreover, one of the most striking characteristics of the world today is *futility*: I may say, with no risk of being too harsh, that we are torn between futility and anxiety. We have the finest playthings man has ever possessed: the motorcar, the yo-yo, the radio, and the cinema; we have everything that genius could create for transmitting, with the speed of light, things not always of the highest quality. What amusements—never so many toys! But what anxieties—never so many alarms!

And lastly, what chores! Chores concealed in comfort itself! Chores that from day to day are only multiplied by our efficiency and our concern for the morrow; for we are caught by the ever more perfect organization of life in an ever tighter net of rules and constraints, many of which we never notice! We are by no means aware of all the things we obey. The telephone rings, we hurry to it; the clock strikes, an appointment calls us . . . . Think of the work schedules, the timetables, the growing demands of hygiene, even the standardization of spelling, which used not to exist, even regulated street crossings; and think what they mean in terms of their effect on the mind . . . . Everything commands us, everything puts pressure on us, everything prescribes what we have to do and tells us to do it automatically. Testing our reflexes has become the important test of the day.

Even the fashion industries have put fantasy under discipline, under *regulations* to control copying, whereby the secret schemes of business rule the aesthetics of the day.

In short, in every way we are circumscribed, dominated by a hidden or obvious regimentation extending to everything, and we are so bewildered by the chaos of stimuli obsessing us that *we end by needing it*.

Are these not detestable conditions for the future production of works of art comparable to those which humanity has created in preceding centuries? We have lost the *leisure to ripen*, and if we look into ourselves as artists, we no longer find that other virtue of our predecessors in the creation of beauty: the aim to endure. Of the many beliefs I have said were dying, one is already gone: that is the belief in posterity and its judgment.

We are now at the end of this review of disorder, which has been rapid and perforce without order. Perhaps you are expecting me to draw some conclusion. We like a play to end happily, or at least to end. You shall have prompt satisfaction on the latter point. For the other, I repeat that my subject is precisely the impossibility of concluding. The need for a conclusion is so strong in us that we irresistibly and absurdly import conclusions into history and even into politics. We cut out patterns of events to make well-rounded tragedies; we want a war, when it ends, to have a clear-cut ending. There is no need for me to tell you that unfortunately this desire is illusory. We believe, too, that a revolution is a clear solution, and we know that this is not true either. These are but crude oversimplifications . . . .

The only conclusion to a study of this kind, to this glimpse of chaos, the only conclusion that might be desirable would be a prediction or presentiment of some sort of future. But I abhor prophesying. Some time ago someone came and asked me what I augured of life and what I thought things would be like in fifty years. As I shrugged my shoulders, the questioner lowered his sights and his prices, and said: "Well, where shall we be in twenty years?" I replied: "*We are backing into the future,*" and I added: "How much could anyone have foreseen in 1882, or 1892, of what has happened since that time? In 1882, fifty years ago, it was impossible to foresee the events and discoveries that have profoundly transformed the face of the earth." And I added, further: "Sir, in 1892 would you have foreseen that in 1932, in order to cross a street in Paris, you would have to seek the protection of a six-month-old baby—negotiate a street-crossing under the safe-conduct of an infant?" He replied: "No, that is something I shouldn't have foreseen either."

In short, more and more it is becoming useless and even dangerous to make predictions based on evidence from yesterday or the day before; but it is still wise, and this will be my last word, to be ready for anything, or almost anything. We must keep in our minds and hearts the will to lucid understanding and precision of mind, a sense of greatness and risk, a sense of the extraordinary adventure on which mankind has set out, departing perhaps too far from the primary and natural conditions of his species, and headed I know not where!

APHORISMS

Albert Einstein

ONE THING I have learned in a long life: that all our science, measured against reality, is primitive and childlike—and yet it is the most precious thing we have.

The supreme task of the physicist is to arrive at those universal elementary laws from which the cosmos can be built up by pure deduction. There is no logical path to these laws; only intuition, resting on sympathetic understanding, can lead to them. . . . The longing to behold [cosmic] harmony is the source of the inexhaustible patience and perseverance. . . . The state of mind that enables a man to do work of this kind is akin to that of the religious worshiper or the lover; the daily effort comes from no deliberate intention or program, but straight from the heart.

It seems to me that the idea of a personal God is an anthropological concept which I cannot take seriously. I feel also not able to imagine some will or goal outside the human sphere. My views are near those of Spinoza: admiration for the beauty of and belief in the logical simplicity of the order and harmony which we can grasp humbly and only imperfectly. I believe that we have to content ourselves with our imperfect knowledge and understanding and treat values and moral obligations as a purely human problem—the most important of all human problems.

God is subtle, but he is not malicious.

God does not throw dice.

To inquire after the meaning or object of one's own existence or that of all creatures has always seemed to me absurd from an objective point of view. And yet everybody has certain ideals which determine the direction of his endeavors and his judgments. In this sense I have never looked upon ease and happiness as ends in themselves—this ethical basis I call the ideal of a pigsty. The ideals which have lighted my way, and time after time have given me courage to face life cheerfully, have been Kindness, Beauty, and Truth. Without the sense of kinship with men of like mind, without the occupation with the objective world, the eternally unattainable in the field of art and scientific endeavors, life would have seemed to me empty. The trite objects of human efforts—possessions, outward success, luxury—have always seemed to me contemptible.

The most beautiful experience we can have is the mysterious. It is the fundamental emotion which stands at the cradle of true art and true science. Whoever does not know it and can no longer wonder, no longer marvel, is as good as dead, and his eyes are dimmed. It was the experience of mystery—even if mixed with fear—that engendered religion. A knowledge of the existence of something we cannot penetrate, our perceptions of the profoundest reason and the most radiant beauty, which only in their most primitive forms are accessible to our minds—it is this knowledge and this emotion that constitute true religiosity; in this sense, and in this alone, I am a deeply religious man. I cannot conceive of a God who rewards and punishes his creatures, or has a will of the kind that we experience in ourselves. Neither can I nor would I want to conceive of an individual that survives his physical death; let feeble souls, from fear or absurd egoism, cherish such thoughts. I am satisfied with the mystery of the eternity of life and with the awareness and a glimpse of the marvelous structure of the existing world, together with the devoted striving to comprehend a portion, be it ever so tiny, of the Reason that manifests itself in nature.

To punish me for my contempt for authority, Fate made me an authority myself.

In the light of knowledge attained, the happy achievement seems almost a matter of course, and any intelligent student can grasp it without too much trouble. But the years of anxious searching in the dark, with their intense longing, their alternations of confidence and exhaustion, and the final emergence into the light—only those who have themselves experienced it can understand that.

What has perhaps been overlooked is the irrational, the inconsistent, the droll, even the insane, which nature, inexhaustively operative, implants in an individual, seemingly for her own amusement. But these things are singled out only in the crucible of one's own mind.

For us believing physicists the distinction between past, present, and future is only an illusion, even if a stubborn one.

The most incomprehensible thing about the world is that it is comprehensible.

THE CREATION

From the Book of Genesis

IN the beginning God created the heaven and the earth. And the earth was without form, and void; and darkness was upon the face of the deep. And the Spirit of God moved upon the face of the waters. And God said, Let there be light: and there was light. And God saw the light, that it was good: and God divided the light from the darkness. And God called the light Day, and the darkness he called Night. And the evening and the morning were the first day.

And God said, Let there be a firmament in the midst of the waters, and let it divide the waters from the waters. And God made the firmament, and divided the waters which were under the firmament from the waters which were above the firmament: and it was so. And God called the firmament Heaven. And the evening and the morning were the second day.

And God said, Let the waters under the heaven be gathered together unto one place, and let the dry land appear: and it was so. And God called the dry land Earth; and the gathering together of the waters called he Seas: and God saw that it was good. And God said, Let the earth bring forth grass, the herb yielding seed, and the fruit tree yielding fruit after his kind, whose seed is in itself, upon the earth: and it was so. And the earth brought forth grass, and herb yielding seed after his kind, and the tree yielding fruit, whose seed was in itself, after his kind: and God saw that it was good. And the evening and the morning were the third day.

And God said, Let there be lights in the firmament of the heaven to divide the day from the night; and let them be for signs, and for seasons, and for days, and years: and let them be for lights in the firmament of the heaven to give light upon the earth: and it was so. And God made two great lights; the greater light to rule the day, and the lesser light to rule the night: he made the stars also. And

God set them in the firmament of the heaven to give light upon the earth, and to rule over the day and over the night, and to divide the light from the darkness: and God saw that it was good. And the evening and the morning were the fourth day.

And God said, Let the waters bring forth abundantly the moving creature that hath life, and fowl that may fly above the earth in the open firmament of heaven. And God created great whales, and every living creature that moveth, which the waters brought forth abundantly, after their kind, and every winged fowl after his kind: and God saw that it was good. And God blessed them, saying, Be fruitful, and multiply, and fill the waters in the seas, and let fowl multiply in the earth. And the evening and the morning were the fifth day.

And God said, Let the earth bring forth the living creature after his kind, cattle, and creeping thing, and beast of the earth after his kind: and it was so. And God made the beast of the earth after his kind, and cattle after their kind, and every thing that creepeth upon the earth after his kind: and God saw that it was good.

And God said, Let us make man in our image, after our likeness: and let them have dominion over the fish of the sea, and over the fowl of the air, and over the cattle, and over all the earth, and over every creeping thing that creepeth upon the earth. So God created man in his own image, in the image of God created he him; male and female created he them. And God blessed them, and God said unto them, Be fruitful, and multiply, and replenish the earth, and subdue it: and have dominion over the fish of the sea, and over the fowl of the air, and over every living thing that moveth upon the earth.

And God said, Behold, I have given you every herb bearing seed, which is upon the face of all the earth, and every tree, in the which is the fruit of a tree yielding seed; to you it shall be for meat. And to every beast of the earth, and to every fowl of the air, and to every thing that creepeth upon the earth, wherein there is life, I have given every green herb for meat: and it was so. And God saw every thing that he had made, and, behold, it was very good. And the evening and the morning were the sixth day.

Thus the heavens and the earth were finished,

and all the host of them. And on the seventh day God ended his work which he had made; and he rested on the seventh day from all his work which he had made. And God blessed the seventh day, and sanctified it: because that in it he had rested from all his work which God created and made.

THE NIGHTINGALE

Hans Christian Andersen

THE EMPEROR of China is a Chinaman, as you most likely know, and everyone around him is a Chinaman too. It's been a great many years since this story happened in China, but that's all the more reason for telling it before it gets forgotten.

The Emperor's palace was the wonder of the world. It was made entirely of fine porcelain, extremely expensive but so delicate that you could touch it only with the greatest of care. In the garden the rarest flowers bloomed, and to the prettiest ones were tied little silver bells which tinkled so that no one could pass by without noticing them. Yes, all things were arranged according to plan in the Emperor's garden, though how far and wide it extended not even the gardener knew. If you walked on and on, you came to a fine forest where the trees were tall and the lakes were deep. The forest ran down to the deep blue sea, so close that tall ships could sail under the branches of the trees. In these trees a nightingale lived. His song was so ravishing that even the poor fisherman, who had much else to do, stopped to listen on the nights when he went out to cast his nets, and heard the nightingale.

"How beautiful that is," he said, but he had his work to attend to, and he would forget the bird's song. But the next night, when he heard the song he would again say, "How beautiful."

From all the countries in the world travelers came to the city of the Emperor. They admired the city. They admired the palace and its garden, but when they heard the nightingale they said, "That is the best of all."

And the travelers told of it when they came home, and men of learning wrote many books about the town, about the palace, and about the garden. But they did not forget the nightingale. They praised him highest of all, and those who were poets wrote magnificent poems about the nightingale who lived in the forest by the deep sea.

These books went all the world over, and some of

them came even to the Emperor of China. He sat in his golden chair and read, and read, nodding his head in delight over such glowing descriptions of his city, and palace, and garden. *But the nightingale is the best of all.* He read it in print.

"What's this?" the Emperor exclaimed. "I don't know of any nightingale. Can there be such a bird in my empire—in my own garden—and I not know it? To think that I should have to learn of it out of a book."

Thereupon he called his Lord-in-Waiting, who was so exalted that when anyone of lower rank dared speak to him, or ask him a question, he only answered, "P," which means nothing at all.

"They say there's a most remarkable bird called the nightingale," said the Emperor. "They say it's the best thing in all my empire. Why haven't I been told about it?"

"I've never heard the name mentioned," said the Lord-in-Waiting. "He hasn't been presented at court."

"I command that he appear before me this evening, and sing," said the Emperor. "The whole world knows my possessions better than I do!"

"I never heard of him before," said the Lord-in-Waiting. "But I shall look for him. I'll find him."

But where? The Lord-in-Waiting ran upstairs and downstairs, through all the rooms and corridors, but no one he met with had ever heard tell of the nightingale. So the Lord-in-Waiting ran back to the Emperor, and said it must be a story invented by those who write books. "Your Imperial Majesty would scarcely believe how much of what is written is fiction, if not downright black art."

"But the book I read was sent me by the mighty Emperor of Japan," said the Emperor. "Therefore it can't be a pack of lies. I must hear this nightingale. I insist upon his being here this evening. He has my high imperial favor, and if he is not forthcoming I will have the whole court punched in the stomach, directly after supper."

"Tsing-pe!" said the Lord-in-Waiting, and off he scurried up the stairs, through all the rooms and corridors. And half the court ran with him, for no one wanted to be punched in the stomach after supper.

There was much questioning as to the whereabouts of this remarkable nightingale, who was so well known everywhere in the world except at home. At last they found a poor little kitchen girl, who said:

"The nightingale? I know him well. Yes, indeed he can sing. Every evening I get leave to carry scraps from the table to my sick mother. She lives down by the shore. When I start back I am tired, and rest in the woods. Then I hear the nightingale sing. It brings tears to my eyes. It's as if my mother were kissing me."

"Little kitchen girl," said the Lord-in-Waiting. "I'll have you appointed scullion for life. I'll even get permission for you to watch the Emperor dine, if you'll take us to the nightingale who is commanded to appear at court this evening."

So they went into the forest where the nightingale usually sang. Half the court went along. On the way to the forest a cow began to moo.

"Oh," cried a courtier, "that must be it. What a powerful voice for a creature so small. I'm sure I've heard her sing before."

"No, that's the cow lowing," said the little kitchen girl. "We still have a long way to go."

The the frogs in the marsh began to croak.

"Glorious!" said the Chinese court parson. "Now I hear it—like church bells ringing."

"No, that's the frogs," said the little kitchen girl. "But I think we shall hear him soon."

Then the nightingale sang.

"That's it," said the little kitchen girl. "Listen, listen, listen! And yonder he sits." She pointed to a little gray bird high up in the branches.

"Is it possible?" cried the Lord-in-Waiting. "Well, I never would have thought he looked like that, so unassuming. But he has probably turned pale at seeing so many important people around him."

"Little nightingale," the kitchen girl called to him, "our gracious Emperor wants to hear you sing."

"With the greatest of pleasure," answered the nightingale, and burst into song.

"Very similar to the sound of glass bells," said the Lord-in-Waiting. "Just see his little throat, how busily it throbs. I'm astounded that we have never heard him before. I'm sure he'll be a great success at court."

"Shall I sing to the Emperor again?" asked the nightingale, for he thought that the Emperor was present.

"My good little nightingale," said the Lord-in-

Waiting, "I have the honor to command your presence at a court function this evening, where you'll delight His Majesty the Emperor with your charming song."

"My song sounds best in the woods," said the nightingale, but he went with them willingly when he heard it was the Emperor's wish.

The palace had been especially polished for the occasion. The porcelain walls and floors shone in the rays of many gold lamps. The flowers with tinkling bells on them had been brought into the halls, and there was such a commotion of coming and going that all the bells chimed away until you could scarcely hear yourself talk.

In the middle of the great throne room, where the Emperor sat, there was a golden perch for the nightingale. The whole court was there, and they let the little kitchen girl stand behind the door, now that she had been appointed "Imperial Pot-Walloper." Everyone was dressed in his best, and all stared at the little gray bird to which the Emperor graciously nodded.

And the nightingale sang so sweetly that tears came into the Emperor's eyes and rolled down his cheeks. Then the nightingale sang still more sweetly, and it was the Emperor's heart that melted. The Emperor was so touched that he wanted his own golden slipper hung round the nightingale's neck, but the nightingale declined it with thanks. He had already been amply rewarded.

"I have seen tears in the Emperor's eyes," he said. "Nothing could surpass that. An Emperor's tears are strangely powerful. I have my reward." And he sang again, gloriously.

"It's the most charming coquetry we ever heard," said the ladies-in-waiting. And they took water in their mouths so they could gurgle when anyone spoke to them, hoping to rival the nightingale. Even the lackeys and chambermaids said they were satisfied, which was saying a great deal, for they were the hardest to please. Unquestionably the nightingale was a success. He was to stay at court, and have his own cage. He had permission to go for a walk twice a day, and once a night. Twelve footmen attended him, each one holding tight to a ribbon tied to the bird's leg. There wasn't much fun in such outings.

The whole town talked about the marvelous bird,

and if two people met, one could scarcely say "night" before the other said "gale," and then they would sigh in unison, with no need for words. Eleven pork-butchers' children were named "Nightingale," but not one could sing.

One day the Emperor received a large package labeled "The Nightingale."

"This must be another book about my celebrated bird," he said. But it was not a book. In the box was a work of art, an artificial nightingale most like the real one except that it was encrusted with diamonds, rubies and sapphires. When it was wound, the artificial bird could sing one of the nightingale's songs while it wagged its glittering gold and silver tail. Round its neck hung a ribbon inscribed: "The Emperor of Japan's nightingale is a poor thing compared with that of the Emperor of China."

"Isn't that nice?" everyone said, and the man who had brought the contraption was immediately promoted to be "Imperial-Nightingale-Fetcher-in-Chief."

"Now let's have them sing together. What a duet that will be," said the courtiers.

So they had to sing together, but it didn't turn out

so well, for the real nightingale sang whatever came into his head while the imitation bird sang by rote.

"That's not the newcomer's fault," said the music master. "He keeps perfect time, just as I have taught him."

Then they had the imitation bird sing by itself. It met with the same success as the real nightingale, and besides it was much prettier to see, all sparkling like bracelets and breastpins. Three and thirty times it sang the selfsame song without tiring. The courtiers would gladly have heard it again, but the Emperor said the real nightingale should now have his turn. Where was he? No one had noticed him flying out the open window, back to his home in the green forest.

"But what made him do that?" said the Emperor.

All the courtiers slandered the nightingale, whom they called a most ungrateful wretch. "Luckily we have the best bird," they said, and made the imitation one sing again. That was the thirty-fourth time they had heard the same tune, but they didn't quite know it by heart because it was a difficult piece. And the music master praised the artificial bird beyond measure. Yes, he said that the contraption was much better than the real nightingale, not only in its dress and its many beautiful diamonds, but also in its mechanical interior.

"You see, ladies and gentlemen, and above all Your Imperial Majesty, with a real nightingale one never knows what to expect, but with this artificial bird everything goes according to plan. Nothing is left to chance. I can explain it and take it to pieces, and show how the mechanical wheels are arranged, how they go around, and how one follows after another."

"Those are our sentiments exactly," said they all, and the music master was commanded to have the bird give a public concert next Sunday. The Emperor said that his people should hear it. And hear it they did, with as much pleasure as if they had all gotten tipsy on tea, Chinese fashion. Everyone said, "Oh," and held up the finger we call "lickpot," and nodded his head. But the poor fishermen who had heard the real nightingale said, "This is very pretty, very nearly the real thing, but not quite. I can't imagine what's lacking."

The real nightingale had been banished from the land. In its place, the artificial bird sat on a cushion beside the Emperor's bed. All its gold and jeweled presents lay about it, and its title was now "Grand Imperial Singer-of-the-Emperor-to-Sleep." In rank it stood first from the left, for the Emperor gave preëminence to the left side because of the heart. Even an Emperor's heart is on the left.

The music master wrote a twenty-five volume book about the artificial bird. It was learned, long-winded, and full of hard Chinese words, yet everybody said they had read and understood it, lest they show themselves stupid and would then have been punched in their stomachs.

After a year the Emperor, his court, and all the other Chinamen knew every twitter of the artificial song by heart. They liked it all the better now that they could sing it themselves. Which they did. The street urchins sang, "Zizizi! kluk, kluk, kluk," and the Emperor sang it too. That's how popular it was.

But one night, while the artificial bird was singing his best by the Emperor's bed, something inside the bird broke with a twang. *Whir-r-r*, all the wheels ran down and the music stopped. Out of bed jumped the Emperor and sent for his own physician, but what could he do? Then he sent for a watchmaker, who conferred, and investigated, and patched up the bird after a fashion. But the watchmaker said that the bird must be spared too much exertion, for the cogs were badly worn and if he replaced them it would spoil the tune. This was terrible. Only once a year could they let the bird sing, and that was almost too much for it. But the music master made a little speech full of hard Chinese words which meant that the bird was as good as it ever was. So that made it as good as ever.

Five years passed by, and a real sorrow befell the whole country. The Chinamen loved their Emperor, and now he fell ill. Ill unto death, it was said. A new Emperor was chosen in readiness. People stood in the palace street and asked the Lord-in-Waiting how it went with their Emperor.

"P," said he, and shook his head.

Cold and pale lay the Emperor in his great magnificent bed. All the courtiers thought he was dead, and went to do homage to the new Emperor. The lackeys went off to trade gossip, and the chambermaids gave a coffee party because it was such a special occasion. Deep mats were laid in all the rooms and passageways, to muffle each footstep. It was quiet in the palace, dead quiet. But the Emperor was not yet dead. Stiff and pale he lay, in his magnificent bed with the long velvet curtains and the heavy gold tassels. High in the wall was an open window, through which moonlight fell on the Emperor and his artificial bird.

The poor Emperor could hardly breathe. It was as if something were sitting on his chest. Opening his eyes he saw it was Death who sat there, wearing the Emperor's crown, handling the Emperor's gold sword, and carrying the Emperor's silk banner. Among the folds of the great velvet curtains there were strangely familiar faces. Some were horrible, others gentle and kind. They were the Emperor's deeds, good and bad, who came back to him now that Death sat on his heart.

"Don't you remember—?" they whispered one after the other. "Don't you remember—?" And they told him of things that made the cold sweat run on his forehead.

"No, I will not remember!" said the Emperor. "Music, music, sound the great drum of China lest I hear what they say!" But they went on whispering, and Death nodded, Chinese fashion, at every word.

"Music, music!" the Emperor called. "Sing, my precious little golden bird, sing! I have given you gold and precious presents. I have hung my golden slipper around your neck. Sing, I pray you, sing!"

But the bird stood silent. There was no one to wind it, nothing to make it sing. Death kept staring through his great hollow eyes, and it was quiet, deadly quiet.

Suddenly, through the window came a burst of song. It was the little live nightingale who sat outside on a spray. He had heard of the Emperor's plight, and had come to sing of comfort and hope. As he sang, the phantoms grew pale, and still more pale, and the blood flowed quicker and quicker through the Emperor's feeble body. Even Death listened, and said, "Go on, little nightingale, go on!"

"But," said the little nightingale, "will you give back that sword, that banner, that Emperor's crown?"

And Death gave back these treasures for a song. The nightingale sang on. It sang of the quiet churchyard where white roses grow, where the elder flowers make the air sweet, and where the grass is always green, wet with the tears of those who are still alive.

Death longed for his garden. Out through the windows drifted a cold gray mist, as Death departed.

"Thank you, thank you!" the Emperor said. "Little bird from Heaven, I know you of old. I banished you once from my land, and yet you have sung away the evil faces from my bed, and Death from my heart. How can I repay you?"

"You have already rewarded me," said the nightingale. "I brought tears to your eyes when first I sang for you. To the heart of a singer those are more precious than any precious stone. But sleep now, and grow fresh and strong while I sing." He sang on until the Emperor fell into a sound, refreshing sleep, a sweet and soothing slumber.

The sun was shining in his window when the Emperor awoke, restored and well. Not one of his servants had returned to him, for they thought him dead, but the nightingale still sang.

"You must stay with me always," said the Emperor. "Sing to me only when you please. I shall break the artificial bird into a thousand pieces."

"No," said the nightingale. "It did its best. Keep it near you. I cannot build my nest here, or live in a palace, so let me come as I will. Then I shall sit on the spray by your window, and sing things that will make you happy and thoughtful too. I'll sing about those who are gay, and those who are sorrowful. My songs will tell you of all the good and evil that you do not see. A little singing bird flies far and wide, to the fisherman's hut, to the farmer's home, and to many other places a long way off from you and your court. I love your heart better than I do your crown, and yet the crown has been blessed too. I will come and sing to you, if you will promise me one thing."

"All that I have is yours," cried the Emperor, who stood in his imperial robes, which he had put on himself, and held his heavy gold sword to his heart.

"One thing only," the nightingale asked. "You must not let anyone know that you have a little bird who tells you everything; then all will go even better." And away he flew.

The servants came in to look after their dead Emperor—and there they stood. And the Emperor said, "Good morning."

FAIRY TALES FOR COMPUTERS

has been set in Monotype Bembo, a fine Venetian face first used by the great printer-scholar of the Renaissance, Aldus Manutius, for the printing of Cardinal Pietro Bembo's *De Aetna* of 1495. The characters were cut by Francesco Griffo who later cut the first italic type, based upon the designs of the Renaissance writing master, Giovantine Tagliente. ❦ This book was manufactured by Murray Printing Company, smyth sewn in signatures, and printed on Warren's Sebago, an entirely acid-free sheet. ❦ Cover design by Cynthia Krupat.